The Seine Was Red

Paris, October 1961

Leïla Sebbar

TRANSLATED BY MILDRED MORTIMER

Indiana University Press

BLOOMINGTON AND INDIANAPOLIS

This text is published with the support of the French Ministry of Culture—National Book Center.

Ouvrage publié avec le concours du Ministère français chargé de la culture—Centre national du livre.

This book is a publication of

Indiana University Press
601 North Morton Street
Bloomington, IN 47404-3797 USA

http://iupress.indiana.edu

Telephone orders   800-842-6796
Fax orders   812-855-7931
Orders by e-mail   iuporder@indiana.edu

Originally published as *La Seine était rouge (Paris, octobre 1961)*
© 1999, 2003 Éditions Thierry Magnier
English translation © 2008 by Indiana University Press
All rights reserved

The paper used in this publication meets the minimum requirements of American National Standard for Information Sciences—Permanence of Paper for Printed Library Materials, ANSI Z39.48-1984.

Manufactured in the United States of America

Library of Congress Cataloging-in-Publication Data

Sebbar, Leïla.
    [Seine était rouge. English]
    The Seine was red : Paris, October 1961 / Leïla Sebbar ; translated by Mildred Mortimer.
        p.   cm.
    Includes bibliographical references.
    ISBN 978-0-253-35246-0 (cloth : alk. paper) — ISBN 978-0-253-22023-3 (pbk. : alk. paper) 1. Algerians—France—Paris—Fiction. 2. Paris (France)—Ethnic relations—Fiction. 3. Riots—France—Paris—Fiction. 4. Police misconduct—France—Paris—Fiction. 5. Jabhat al-Tahrir al-Qawmi—Fiction. I. Mortimer, Mildred P. II. Title.
    PQ2679.E244S4513 2008
    843'.914—dc22
                                                                    2008019742

1 2 3 4 5   13 12 11 10 09 08

To the Algerian victims of October 1961 in Paris

To the Maurice Audin Committee

To Didier Daeninckx
Jean-Luc Einaudi
Elie Kagan
Nacer Kettane
Mehdi Lallaoui
François Maspéro
Georges Mattei
Jacques Panijel
Paulette Péju
Anne Tristan

—LEÏLA SEBBAR

Paris, October 1961

Contents

Acknowledgments

I would like to thank Leïla Sebbar for her inspiring literary texts and her willingness to share her thoughts about this novel and her other work with me. I am also grateful to Dee Mortensen and Laura MacLeod at Indiana University Press for encouraging me at every step of this translation project. I thank critics Michel Laronde and Anne Donadey for their insightful studies of *La Seine était rouge,* critical explorations that preceded "Unearthing Hidden History," my introduction to the novel. Finally, I thank Anne Donadey for her careful reading of this translation and pertinent suggestions.

Introduction:
Unearthing Hidden History

Mildred Mortimer

If the process of reflecting upon the legacy of French colonialism leads to the reexamination of colonial history, it often results in the reinterpretation of historical events. Since colonial administrations would, at times, misrepresent colonial history to justify an imperial project, it is not surprising that postcolonial writers, following the path taken by historians, have assumed the task of rewriting their nation's colonial history. Hence, the theme of the hidden history—the colonial cover-up—has become increasingly important in postcolonial literature, and has led to significant discoveries. In this vein, when Algerian novelist, Assia Djebar, delved into French colonial history pertaining to the conquest of Algeria, she uncovered a "forgotten" incident of *enfumade*, the French military tactic of setting caves on fire to asphyxiate Algerian tribes taking refuge in them. Djebar came to view herself as a spelunker, an underground explorer engaged in "a very special kind of speleology." (1985, 77). Leïla Sebbar, in turn, entered this realm, by examining more recent hidden history, a cover-up that occurred as the French occupation of Algeria drew to a close. Her speleological endeavor involves the massacre of Algerians in Paris on October 17, 1961.

The basic facts that constitute the events of October 17, 1961 are now known. In October 1961, the Algerian FLN (Front de Libération Nationale) organized a peaceful demonstration of Algerians in Paris to protest a curfew imposed upon them by the head of the Paris police at the time, Maurice Papon, a man who had been a Nazi collaborator during World War II and who died in February 2007. He had ordered the curfew to control the movements of Algerians living in France whom he considered to be FLN sympathizers and supporters. Occurring during the final months of the Algerian war, the protest march turned violent when the Paris police attacked the Algerians demonstrating peacefully.[1] It is now estimated that 30,000 Algerian men, women, and children took part in the demonstration (Einaudi 1991, 183). The estimated number of Algerians killed varies between 200 and 300 people (ibid., 14; Laronde 2007, 142). Many of the dead perished in the Seine. Others disappeared, their bodies dumped in the woods around Paris. Still others, survivors of the massacre, were deported to Algeria where they remained prisoners in camps until the end of the war, or were sent back to their home villages. Despite the extent of the violence, the massacres were largely kept out of the French press at the time. Michel Laronde calls this cover-up an *acte forclos*, an action that has been deliberately placed beyond the realm of official history by institutional silence (Laronde 2007, 147).

Sebbar is neither the first nor the only novelist to examine the massacre and the silence that surrounded it. In fact, at the beginning of *La Seine était rouge,* she acknowledges the other writers who preceded her in this endeavor: Didier Daeninckx, *Meurtres pour mémoire,* 1984; Nacer Kettane, *Le sourire de Brahim,* 1985; Mehdi Lallaoui, *Les beurs de Seine,* 1986; Georges Mattei, *La guerre des gusses,* 1982. She pays tribute to the historians, photographers, and journalists who struggled to bring this hidden chapter of French history to light as well. Sebbar is, however, the first to use the historical event as the entire subject of a novel (Donadey 2003, 190).

The novelist's relationship to Algerian history and literature is unique. The daughter of an Algerian father and a French mother, Sebbar spent her formative years in Algeria and her adult life in France. Identifying herself as a *croisée*, a hybrid at the intersection of Occidental and Oriental cultures, she writes primarily about North African immigrant society in France.[2] Although she first used writing to re-create the world of marginalized immigrants in order to lessen her own personal sense of exile, she has recently moved in a new direction, probing personal and collective memories of Algeria at the end of the colonial era. This 'speleological endeavor' has resulted in autobiographical texts such as *Je ne parle pas la langue de mon père*, 2003, and *Mes Algéries en France*, 2004.

Sebbar comes to the events of October 17, 1961 indirectly; she was in neither Paris nor Algeria at the time of the massacre, and explains:

> I was in Aix-en-Provence, where I had forgotten Algeria. This amnesia lasted a long time. France represented freedom. I could finally live without the fear of war, without surveillance, without protection.[3]

The novelist arrived at the writing project indirectly as well. It was suggested to her by Algerian sociologist, Abdelkader Djeghloul, who, in 1990, edited an issue of *Actualité de l'émigration hébdo*, commemorating the events of October 17, 1961. Her contribution, a three-page text, "La Seine était rouge," ["The Seine Was Red"] initiated her reflections upon the importance of an event which, until then, she had never examined.

The short piece begins with the writer's memories associated with the fateful day. Sebbar expresses feelings of distance from both Paris and Algeria, then evokes her sentiment of unease in Aix-en-Provence where, sequestered in her student room, she hears a voice on the radio announcing the October 17 demonstration. Almost three decades later, she recalls: "I am alone, reclusive, and seated in this armchair from which I don't stir, I am listening to the violent and memorable history that is taking place while I am seated there" (1998, 96).[4]

A writer who has always insisted upon the importance of both personal and collective memory, Sebbar, in these few pages, reveals the importance of image and sound to the process of restoring memory. In 1986, while examining a newspaper photo, she finds that the image brings back the sounds and voices associated with past events of October 17, 1961. Thus, this short text that shares its title with the novel published almost ten years later, marks the beginning of the novelist's quest for clarity and understanding with respect to the violent repression, and helps explain why she chose to write this novel as an *anamnesis* or collective memory of the events surrounding the massacre.[5]

Using a collective process of diverse eyewitness accounts, the novel presents differing points of view. Hence, French policemen, their Algerian collaborators, Algerian demonstrators, French supporters of the Algerian cause, and other diverse individuals all give their perspective on the events. By situating her novel thirty-five years after the event, Sebbar emphasizes the importance of rewriting history while admitting the difficulties involved in establishing the truth through memory. Indeed, in the text, a middle-aged Frenchman, questioned thirty years after the events that occurred when he was a young student in Paris, admits that his memory has

weakened with time; "I have already forgotten the dates . . .
My memory is weak," he notes (p. 82).

Setting her novel in 1996, Sebbar introduces three main
characters who had not yet been born when the events of October 17, 1961 took place. Amel, a sixteen-year-old teenager, is
the daughter of Algerian immigrants. Omer, a twenty-seven-
year-old journalist, is living in exile in France because of the
violence in Algeria in the 1990s. Louis, twenty-five, is French.
He has decided to make a documentary film concerning the
massacre, thereby contributing his efforts to breaking the silence to which both the victims of the violence and their per-
petrators have contributed. Through her choice of protagonists, the novelist focuses on the three principal groups for
whom *anamnesis* is crucial: Algerian immigrants in France,
Algerians fleeing strife at home, French partisans of Algerian independence. Significantly, their connection is through
their mothers, women who had become close friends during
that period. Amel's mother, Noria, and grandmother, Lalla,
Omer's mother, Mina, and Louis's mother, Flora, all participated in Algeria's struggle for independence.

Although these women forged lasting friendships through
a common political struggle that marked their lives, they are
reticent about sharing this part of their past with their children. Hence, their children, faced with their mothers' silence
and unable to truly understand the reasons for it, find themselves compelled to search for traces of a hidden story, traces
they will find in Paris in the late 1990s.

Why are the women silent? Sebbar proposes two answers. First, "One doesn't speak of painful things."[6] Simply
stated, the women do not want to return to traumatic events
that caused them pain and suffering and transmit this legacy
to the next generation. Second, Algerian culture had taught

them to distinguish between public and private events, male and female space. They consider the events of October 17 as belonging to the realm of men and their concerns: "the day of men and their politics."[7] Demonstrating alongside the men, these women were clearly supporting the political demonstration but they considered their role to be auxiliary, not central, their own realm being the intimate world of domestic space.

Posing the problem of a previous generation's silence with respect to the events of October 17, 1961, Sebbar initiates a process that will result in her own autobiographical project. In *Je ne parle par la langue de mon père* [*I don't speak my father's native tongue*], published four years later, she probes the silence that weighs upon her own family history, drawing attention to her father's unwillingness to ever engage her in conversation about his experiences in Algeria during the war. He was arrested by the French army in 1957, while serving as a school principal in Algeria, and spent several months in prison in Orléansville.

Although her father might indeed share the women's reluctance to unearth painful memories, he would not share their perspective concerning public space and politics. Sebbar suggests that language may be an important factor contributing to her father's silence. Perhaps her conversations in French, the colonizer's tongue, served to create a communication barrier that otherwise would not have existed. Had she been able to converse with her father in Arabic, his maternal language, she might have been able to reach him: "Perhaps the foreign tongue separated him from the words he would have chosen for us, his children" (Sebbar 2003, 20).

In *The Seine Was Red*, a fictionalized account of historical events in which her father did not participate—he was in Algeria at the time—Sebbar foregrounds the linguistic barrier that prevents her protagonist, Amel, from participating in the Arabic language conversations of her mother and grandmother. As Amel emphasizes the unwillingness of the older generation to share information with the young—"Her mother said nothing to her, nor did her mother's mother" (p. 1)—she notes that both mother and grandmother claim to be withholding information from her temporarily; they propose to reveal this history eventually. Grandmother says: "Secrets, my girl, secrets that you shouldn't know, that must be kept hidden. But you'll learn them some day, when you need to." (p. 1).

Frustrated by their unwillingness to divulge the information she seeks at this moment in time, Amel sets out to complete the official story with unofficial accounts, those not recorded in official archives. To fill in the blanks, to learn this unofficial story, she turns to Louis's film. In this film, she discovers her mother speaking directly into the eye of Louis's camera. A child at the time of the historical event, Amel's mother Noria—now in middle-age—is finally able to articulate the words that childhood trauma had kept buried for years.

Significantly, Noria's process of remembering is mediated through a camera held by an outsider. Here, as Sebbar explains, the principle of psychoanalysis comes into play.[8] Speaking to the eye of the camera, Noria is able to recreate scenes of trauma and evoke her personal, painful sense of loss. Although she cannot yet speak to her daughter, she can bear witness via a different medium. Thus, Sebbar shows that when crucial dialogue between parents and children fails, the message can nevertheless be articulated through other means. In the final analysis, the message—not the means of transmission—matters most.

Revealing the irony that both victims and victimizers

collude to stifle the record of colonial atrocities, Sebbar insists that silence surrounding these events must be broken; stories must be told, *anamnesis* must occur. Yet some victims of traumatic events share Lalla, Noria, Flora, and Mina's reticence. Significantly, Elie Wiesel, the most prominent spokesman for survivors of the Holocaust, has expressed two conflicting views regarding the traumatic history of events that he, a Holocaust survivor, experienced. On the one hand, he believes that it is impossible to communicate an experience to those who have not been through it. Hence, genocide survivors like himself speak first and foremost to other survivors. On the other hand, he insists that memory is the tool for ensuring that barbarous acts will not be forgotten.

For Sebbar's young protagonists, the act of remembering includes erecting monuments to the courageous men, women, and children who participated in Algeria's liberation struggle. Hence, the young people not only encourage their parents to bear witness, they also edit French commemorative plaques that honor fallen World War II heroes, adding citations that proclaim the heroism of Algerian militants.

The first plaque they choose to alter is one they find on the wall of the Santé prison. It reads:

ON NOVEMBRE 11 1940

IN THIS PRISON WERE HELD

HIGH SCHOOL AND UNIVERSITY STUDENTS

WHO, AT THE CALL OF GENERAL DE GAULLE

WERE THE FIRST TO RISE UP

AGAINST THE OCCUPATION (p. 14).

Omer adds bold letters in red paint that read:

1954–1962

IN THIS PRISON

WERE GUILLOTINED

ALGERIAN RESISTERS

WHO ROSE UP

AGAINST THE FRENCH OCCUPATION (p. 15).

By remaining as faithful as possible to the vocabulary and syntax of the original commemorative language, Omer establishes a parallel between both texts and both events. Superimposing their commemorative words in red paint, they pay homage to the martyrs drowned the day that the Seine turned red with Algerian martyrs' blood.

Studying the plaque on the wall of the Santé prison, we note an important resemblance and a crucial difference between the two inscriptions. First, to emphasize the parallel between the two historical events, the plaque informs readers that both the students and the Algerian nationalists were protesting foreign occupation; the French students rose up against one foreign occupier, the Germans; the Algerian nationalists rose up against another, the French colonizers. Second, to emphasize the difference between the two events of heroic resistance to occupation, the plaque informs us that the high school and university students were *imprisoned*, but the Algerian resisters were *guillotined*.

French historian Pierre Nora notes in the introduction to his extensive study of the relationship between history, memory, and memory sites, that *lieux de mémoire*, or places of memory, share three qualities: they are material, symbolic, and functional (1992, xxxiv). For example, war memorials erected in most French villages following World War I reflect these characteristics. They are material, made of stone.

They are symbolic, representing France's loss of almost an entire generation of young men conscripted to serve in the French Army at the time. They are functional, listing the names of each soldier from that village who died in the war. By erecting plaques to commemorate historical events—first the death sentence carried out against Algerian nationalists in the Santé prison, then the homage to victims of the massacre of October 17, 1961—Sebbar's protagonists create their own *lieux de mémoire*. These memory sites are equally material, symbolic, functional. They are durable, the red paint permeating the stone. They are symbolic, representing Algeria's loss of human life. They are functional, reminding all passersby of the historical event.

The altered plaque that links one historical period with another encourages Donadey to attest to the parallel between the *Vichy syndrome* (French historian Henry Rousso's term to designate France's inability to deal with its Vichy past) and the subsequent "syndrome" that Donadey calls the *Algerian syndrome*, a term she uses to define France's inability to deal with its Algerian past. In both cases, the critic notes, the shadowy French functionary Maurice Papon played an important role. Having first ordered the deportation of French Jews to Nazi concentration camps in the Vichy era, then serving in Algeria to destroy the FLN, he subsequently ordered the violent repression of the Algerian demonstration as the Algerian war was drawing to a close (Donadey 2003, 187–194). One of the hand-written notices Omer and Amel scrawl on a hotel façade explicitly condemns Papon for his brutality:

ON THIS SPOT ALGERIANS WERE SAVAGELY BEATEN
BY PREFECT PAPON'S POLICE
OCTOBER 17, 1961 (p. 67).

As the hidden history of repression is brought to light, the date confirmed, and participants such as Papon identified, *anamnesis*, the collective process of remembering, has significant consequences for the individual as well as the community. The quest embarked upon by Amel, Omer, and Louis influences their relationship with one another, their relationship with their parents, and in the case of Amel's mother, her relationship to Louis's camera.

We should note before concluding that the publication of *La Seine était rouge* in 1999 coincided with new commemorative initiatives that honor the victims of the massacre. On May 5, 1999, Prime Minister Lionel Jospin announced that the French government "has decided to facilitate access to public archives dealing with the events of October 17, 1961" (Stora 2003, 26). On June 10, 1999, the French National Assembly recognized the fact that "actions to maintain order" in Algeria from 1954 to 1962 did constitute a war (Donadey 2003, 197). Finally, on October 17, 2001, the mayor of Paris, Bertrand Delanoë, placed a commemorative plaque on the bridge at Saint-Michel honoring the victims of October 17, 1961 (Sebbar 2004, 95). A reminder to passersby of the innocent blood spilled that infamous day, the plaque is dedicated:

IN MEMORY

OF THE MANY ALGERIANS

KILLED DURING THE BLOODY

REPRESSION

OF THE PEACEFUL DEMONSTRATION

ON OCTOBER 17, 1961

The memorial confirms to the French and Algerian public that the infamous day is no longer a blank in history; *anamnesis* is finally beginning to replace amnesia.

What part have literary voices such as Sebbar's played in the commemorative initiatives? By calling attention to injustice, she illustrates the painful history of violence accompanying French colonialism in Algeria, violence that extended to Algerians living in France during the Algerian war. Perhaps most significantly, as she brings this tragic incident and its silencing by French authorities to light, she gives voice to the Algerian immigrant youth living in France, young people who are struggling to come to terms with the past as they seek to find their place in the France of today where cultural diversity remains a goal still to be achieved.

The Seine
Was Red

Nanterre. Amel.

October 1996

Her mother said nothing to her, nor did her mother's mother.

Mother and daughter see each other often. They chat in French and Arabic. Amel doesn't understand everything they say. She hears them from her room. If she were to ask them what they were saying in the other language, "the language of the homeland" as Lalla calls it, her grandmother would say as she always does: "Secrets, my girl, secrets that you shouldn't know, that must be kept hidden. But you'll learn them some day, when you need to. The day will come, don't worry; it will come and it won't be a happy one for you." Amel is persistent: "Why call it a day of woe? Why is the truth a source of woe? Tell me, Lalla, tell me . . . When will I know? Do you and Mom always speak Arabic so that I'm still the little girl who doesn't know the language of the homeland, her mother and father's tongue? If you speak Greek, Classical Greek, of course, I'll understand everything. Are you punishing me because I don't know your native language or speak it so badly you make fun of me?" "Not at all, my child, I'll never punish you for not learning to speak our Ancestors' language; you tried. I tried to teach you; you didn't say no, but you didn't learn to speak Arabic. Your mother, like me, didn't have the time back in our shack in the shantytown . . . You know English, Latin, Greek . . . You are well-educated, my child. I'm not going to punish you for being well-educated . . ." "As for the shantytown, you only told me it was located at the site of the big park or near the university, I don't know, somewhere on the other side of town. Tell me about the shantytown, Nanterre, Mom, and your life . . . there was the war . . . in Algeria, and here too. You told me those years were difficult, but when I ask questions about them, you don't answer." "Later on, my child, much later; I don't feel like talking about it right now. Let's talk about today . . ." "You always say later, later and I learn nothing. You talk to Mom; you could tell me everything, and you say nothing, and Mom says nothing. You keep saying I'm well-educated, but you make fun of me, and I'm kept in the dark. You speak of a secret. What's a secret? Is it so dreadful you have to hide it all?" "All, no, but what's painful, yes. You see, I didn't want to tell you that unhappiness exists, but you force me to . . ." "But I know that, you're not teaching me anything new. We see it every day on TV, we read it, I read it in books . . ." "In books, on TV . . . It's not the same as what I'll tell you someday, when the time is right, and your mother will too." "When the time is right? How will you know when?" "I'll know; that's all."

Amel hears her mother and Lalla talking and laughing. Lalla laughs in her native language, a throaty, voluptuous laugh. It is a strong rolling laugh, slightly guttural, not like her mother's laugh, discreet and less melodious. She likes to listen to them laughing as they talk. Lalla lives with grandfather in a cottage near the university. "Vegetables from back home," her grandfather never calls them by their name, but she knows what he is talking about. The garden is small. Amel would follow the old man with his watering can from one plot to the other, every Sunday. She knows everything there is to know about the vegetables that go into the *chorba*, her favorite soup, Ramadan soup. The old folks—she calls them "the old folks" with tenderness—are preparing for their trip to Mecca. When she said, "You are so old and you are going so far . . ." Lalla answered "To die in Mecca is an honor that Allah grants the faithful" . . . Grandfather agreed. If she leaves, she'll no longer hear them talking about this famous pilgrimage, repeating the names of the cities and the countries they'll cross. The map is tacked on to the dining room wall, above the TV. She'll no longer hear her mother and Lalla's laughter, and their words—secret, foreign.

Nanterre—University—The Regional Metro—Paris.
October 1996.

Paris

If she hadn't met Louis and Omer, Amel would never have known anything. "When the time is right," repeats Lalla. She could die before that day comes. To die during the pilgrimage will grant Lalla entry into paradise, but for her, how will she learn the truth?

Flora and Mina

Louis wasn't home. She should have called him. She doesn't like to call from public phone booths; you're on display . . . like the open stalls of the smelly toilets; in the cafés you can hear everything and the toilet flush muffles the voice . . . She doesn't call.

Flora opened the door. "Amel! What's going on? You're looking glum" . . . "Me? I'm not. Why do you say that?" "I say what I see, that's all and I know I'm right. Do you know how long I've known you? You forget that I was the first to see you, the day you were born, before your father. I was working in the hospital where you were born and your mother, she was barely seven years old when I went to see Lalla . . . But you know all of that by heart, so why am I repeating myself? So, if I say I think you're acting strange, I'm not mistaken, do you understand?" "Yes, but everything is fine." "Are you hungry?" "Yes."

Omer is seated on the sofa, his left hand scratching the

raised geometric pattern of the Aït-Hichem rug that had been woven for Flora. When she was in prison, Flora listened to her cellmates and one of them always said: "If we had a loom, one like our mothers and grandmothers, we would have fun teaching you, Frenchwomen, how to weave, and we would be warm in winter, here . . . Let's draw up a petition for a loom and some wool. Why not? The supervisors will see us busy, doing something useful. Who will think we can plot, organize a hunger strike?" They got salvaged wool and knitting needles to make scarves . . . Flora kept hers, green and red, knitted in moss stitch. She didn't know how to knit . . . She learned the letters of the Arabic alphabet and some Kabyle words. Her cellmate from Aït-Hachem, after their prison days were over, had a rug woven for Flora. Today, her friend Mina said to her: "It may be the last one in the village. You know, Algeria is forgetting its people, and its women weavers . . . Soon they won't know how to weave anymore. Some of the women are weaving for the Gobelins factory in Lodève. They don't teach their daughters in Algeria how to weave. Wool is scarce; it's too expensive; no one wants to pay them for their work, and what work . . . Fine, I'm not going to lament over rugs when men, women, and children are dying, when sons are slitting women's throats—killing their mothers, sisters, cousins—when the army and the police execute, torture . . . I'll stop talking. I don't want to repeat it again and again. It's like madness. With the others, you know, Flora, we were in a struggle, an unequal war against the French army, but the fight seemed just. I believe it was just. It was cruel, but I still think, even today, that we were right. The resistance, prison . . . In Algeria, in France. That's where I met you and also the young French girl from Tlemcen. She was sixteen years old and in the resistance. We would talk, during the day, at night, each one in her native tongue and in the common language, French . . . You were the teacher and also the pupil, like each one of us. We shared the French women's provisions. We read each other's letters . . . Do you remember? You're going to say I'm nostalgic for prison . . . for those days, those weeks we spent together in jail cells; yes I am. There was complicity, friendship, there were discoveries in spite of our disputes . . . Interrogations, threats . . . persecutions, humiliations. I haven't forgotten them, but I never again found that profound, true, sincere solidarity. Today, in spite of the risks of death, the danger of summary executions, I haven't been able to put together those networks of resistance and aid I once knew. Barely threatened, I had to leave . . . And here I am, at your house . . . I know I can stay here as long as I wish, but I'm not in Algeria. I'm not working. An Algerian lawyer in Paris means one more unemployed person, and a clandestine one . . . Omer, whom you have also taken in . . . his situation is worse . . . His father, in Algiers, is threatened, but doesn't want to leave his position at the hospital . . ."

Flora ushers Amel towards the kitchen. She stops near the sofa. The young man folds his newspaper. Flora says: "This is Amel, Noria's daughter, Lalla's granddaughter." "This is Omer, Mina's son, she's the one making the coffee; he's Louis's friend, you know my son, Louis." Omer stood up, shook Amel's hand, a little too hard, sat down, picked up the paper again. He said hello without looking at her. She looked at him. He is tall and thin. His shirt is blue, the color of forget-me-nots, the sleeves are rolled up. His skin is brown, his mustache black. It is thick, like her grandfather's in a photo where he is standing against the factory door. You can see written on the pediment: RENAULT. This is the factory on "the island" as his grandfather would say every time he spoke of what was also called "the jail." She knows her mother went to "the island" when she was seven years old. Her father took her by the hand and they walked into the enormous work-shop where they were making cars on the assembly line. He explained it all to her, patiently. She says that she understood it all. He was proud of the "island" factory, happy to show his daughter "the temple of the French automobile industry," as the foreman called it, until the day when . . . grandfather never said anything more about that infamous day. Omer has the same fleshy mouth. She didn't see the color of his eyes.

Mina kissed her. "I saw a photo of your grandmother. You look like her. Don't you think so, Flora? You know the photo of Lalla at the protest march with her daughter, Noria . . . Do you still have it?" "I think Louis stole all my photos of those years. The Algerian war, October 17, 1961 . . . I can't find them . . ." Flora says to Amel: "Ask Louis for them."

On the doorstep, Amel turns around. Omer is reading the paper. He said goodbye without stirring, from a distance. Flora hugs Amel: "Take care of yourself. I find you strange. Is everything OK at Nanterre? Are you sure?" "Everything is fine and I am too." "I'll call your mother this evening." "If you wish. Bye."

The Seine
Was Red

Louis. Rue de La Santé

Amel rings several times at Number 57, Rue de La Santé.[1] Louis lives on the top floor of an apartment house in the 13th arrondissement. From his balcony, he can see into the prison. Using binoculars, he would be able to follow the prisoners on their daily walks. He didn't intend to rent a two-bedroom apartment with a balcony facing the prison. He inadvertently followed up on an ad and it worked out right away. During his first few months there, he didn't think of spending any time on the balcony, because it was raining. Today, he decides he'll make a short film on La Santé prison as seen from his apartment building. His mother has told him about the women's prisons in which she had been jailed during the Algerian war. The prisons were in the provinces, and in Paris. She said that she had met women there she would never have met otherwise and that she didn't regret the time spent even if . . . She didn't finish her story. Not until the day he said he was going to make a film on the "suitcase couri-

ers,"[2] including the women couriers, he added: "I know that
you aided the Algerians and that Dad did too. He wasn't in
the field in Egypt then. Weren't the excavations interrupted
at that time because of the war? That's what he told me. I
don't know what he did, nor you; the two of you begin to talk
and then you stop; and if I ask you questions, you don't answer them. Why?" His mother smiled: "So, you want to know
everything, everything." "I want to know the truth about
this war." "What truth? You know, the truth . . . That's difficult . . ." "Your truth, Dad's truth, what you thought, experienced, suffered through . . . your life . . ." "But you'll only
have one aspect, a tiny one, and it's too partial . . . More than
thirty-five years ago . . . Imagine . . . We've forgotten; it will
be vague, approximate, uninteresting, I promise . . . Ask your
father, you'll see." "He said yes; he's willing to talk, find archives for me, photos, newspapers, tracts . . . He doesn't mind
me filming him, you see. And you?" His mother hesitated;
"Do you really need to make this film? It isn't your story . . ."
"Exactly, I want to do it. I'll do it because it isn't my story.
1954–1962. October 17, 1961 in Paris and you in this colonial
war . . . You betrayed France, didn't you? You fought with
the Algerians against your country . . . Is that true or not?
I'm saying this knowing you've never been traitors. Don't
worry, Mom. But even so, it bothers me. I need to know, not
everything, but I need to understand some of it. I no longer
know what it means to be a revolutionary, today, at the end
of the 1990s, our years, the end of our century." "Soon it will
be the year 2000. All these stories, Louis, I assure you, won't
interest anyone, except the old men and women who lived
through them and even them, how many of them wish to
forget, and they do forget. Really, think about it. I'm afraid
you're wasting your time. We were young, your father and
I, we were students, we were idealists. I'm not sure we really

gave it much thought." "You sheltered a deserter. I saw his book in the house: *The Deserter*. Who was this deserter?" "Today, I can tell you. He signed it: Maurienne; his name is Jean-Louis Hurst . . . You can meet him for your film, if you wish." "I'll go to see him. You made a commitment. It was dangerous. You risked death, getting caught up in the settling of old scores, an attack. You went to prison. Dad had to go into hiding, and afterwards you were at the Algerian protest march on October 17, 1961 . . . You can't say you didn't think about it. You must say yes; say yes, Mom. You will see. This will be the best film about this chapter in history; say yes." "Yes. But I don't have much time, you know. The hospital schedule . . ." "Do you think I can have your letters?" "Which ones? If they are the letters written by militants, your father has those." "And the others . . ." "What others?" "Your letters . . ." "Oh! Not those . . . our letters, those that your father and I wrote to one another . . . You'll have them when we die . . ." "I was joking." "I know."

Louis made the film. He will be showing it soon at a film festival.

Amel rings the bell once more. No one is home. She heads toward Arago Boulevard. Someone stops her: "Hi! It's Omer . . ." Amel looks at him, smiling into his dark eyes: "I'm Amel. I saw you at Flora's. I know you are Omer. Were you going to see Louis?" "Yes. About his film." "What film? He never said anything to me about it . . . You barely know him; he tells everything to you, nothing to me. He has known me from the day I was born, well almost . . . I've known him forever and he doesn't tell me anything . . . that's really too much . . ." "He wants to surprise you. Maybe we'll see it together." "Well, I won't go unless he invites me, I surely won't."

"Amel! Amel! Omer! Where are you going?"

Louis runs towards them: "Amel, I called you at home; your mother is worried . . . she said that you . . ." Amel interrupts Louis: "That's my problem. Don't say anything to my mother. You didn't see me, and neither did Flora . . ." "What's the matter with you? You are playing the runaway, the rebel, what's up . . . I'm not going to lie to your mother and make my mother lie . . ." "If you say one word, I will never see you again. That's it. If you squeal, it's over." Omer unfolds his newspaper. Louis takes him by the arm: "Let's go." Omer looks up at the high brown walls of La Santé. He reads, above the blue door:

LIBERTY EQUALITY FRATERNITY

He ushers Louis and Amel over to the corner of the prison. He reads aloud the words on the white marble plaque attached to the corner of the prison:

ON NOVEMBER 11 1940
IN THIS PRISON WERE HELD
HIGH SCHOOL AND UNIVERSITY STUDENTS
WHO, AT THE CALL OF GENERAL DE GAULLE,
WERE THE FIRST TO RISE UP
AGAINST THE OCCUPATION

He turns to Louis: "Do you know what I'm going to do? Right away, over there, at your house, since you live in front of the main entrance? Do you have white paper and a felt tipped marker? If not, we can spray bomb graffiti on the wall; that's probably better. It won't come off, etched in the stone . . . Do you have red paint? I'll do it tonight." "What do you want to do?" "You can put it in your film if this story interests you . . ." "You're not going to start lecturing me . . . everyone has a story, a special way of looking at things . . ."

"Yes, but historic truth? I don't want to discuss that now. I just want to acknowledge what happened inside these walls. That was another war. Even if you[3] talked about the 'Events' . . ." "'You' who?" Louis yells. "What do you mean by that? 'You . . . you.' Explain . . ." Amel takes Louis by the arm: "Calm down, Louis. Omer didn't mean . . ." "He said it, he said, 'you, you French . . .' For him all the French . . . My parents were called traitors, and that's all he has to say . . . That's his historical truth."

Louis looks at Omer and Amel: "Bye!"

Omer says to Amel: "You won't see his film today . . ."

Louis films the prison wall, at the corner of Rue de La Santé and Arago Boulevard, with the commemorative plaque fixed to the stone, and on the right of it, red graffiti letters:

1954–1962

IN THIS PRISON

WERE GUILLOTINED

ALGERIAN RESISTERS

WHO ROSE UP

AGAINST THE FRENCH OCCUPATION

The police car passing by doesn't notice anything unusual.

Amel and Omer watch Louis's film several times.

Nanterre. Amel and Omer

They have been walking for two hours across the university campus of Nanterre. They reach the Pierre and Marie Curie library, Amel's other home. Amel is looking for the site of the shantytown called La Folie where her mother had lived. Her mother never said anything about this to her. She has spoken to Louis at length, but to her, never more than a minute and a half . . . And here, her mother talks and talks and talks. She doesn't stop, and she looks straight at Louis while he films her. He focuses particularly on her face. What if she cries . . . Amel closed her eyes for a moment. Don't cry. Her mother's voice. Her mother is beautiful. Lalla says so every time she brushes her daughter's long hair, in front of the old vanity mirror she bought at the Clignancourt flea market. Noria kept it because her mother is attached to it. It was their first piece of furniture in the low-income housing project, after they left the transit housing project. Amel knows her mother is beautiful because people have told her so. Her high school friends say: "Your mother is beautiful! . . ." And her? Well, it's as if . . . And the way her father looks at his wife when he comes home from the factory. A man who loves his wife. Is that so rare?

Amel and Omer walk along the university streets, in the big park. Amel wears a Tibetan cap, dark glasses, a long black raincoat. Omer says to her: "Are you in disguise?" "Yes. I'm disguised as an unknown person. If that bothers you . . ." "No. In Algiers I wore a disguise . . . I got used to it . . ." "You haven't told me why you're here." "Some other time . . ." "You too, like the others, my mother, my father, Lalla and my grandfather: 'When the time is right'"? "I'll tell you one day, not now. But I'll tell you."

Amel hears her mother's voice.

The Mother

"I was little, maybe seven years old. I remember that we lived at number 7. The number 7 was written on the wooden door in white paint. I don't know how the mailman was able to deliver the mail. Streets without names, other streets with weird names, street signs that were often illegible . . . Those streets . . . if you could even call them streets. Ours was called Rue de la Fontaine, because the fountain wasn't far. We didn't have to go several hundred yards for water, like the others who carried their water back in giant milk cans on dollies. You can imagine in the winter, the frost, the rain, the mud. It wasn't too horrible for us, I mean for me. I didn't like the transit housing project. But our shack in the shantytown didn't bother me too much. The shantytown was called La Folie. I don't know why. It was the name of a section of Nanterre, surely a vacant lot before the shacks were built. It's the town where I was born. I can't say I miss it, but I know my mother suffered; she'll tell you she did. I didn't. I don't know about my brothers. We never speak about it.

"I was the only girl, and the youngest. The 'horribly spoiled one' as my mother would say. I have four brothers. The oldest two were born in Algeria, and the others in Nanterre, like me. I think I was my father's favorite; my brothers always called me 'spoiled rotten.' My father would say, 'I'm taking the "little one" with me.' He called me the little one, never Noria. My mother did laundry on afternoons when there was no school. I didn't help her yet, and my father would say to me, 'Let's go, little one.' He would take me by the hand. 'You have such a tiny hand. . . .' He would look at it in his open palm. His hands were big and wide, his skin brown and cracked, 'like the earth at home when the weather has been hot for a long time.' That's what he said every time he squeezed my hand in his. 'There were no fields left for me, yet I knew how to work the land. Your grandfather said to me: "Go across the sea. They say there is work over there. You will send money back for your house here, and you'll marry someone from our village, like I did." I was in the war in Indochina. It's far away, Indochina, and I came back. I came back alive but exhausted. Your grandfather kissed me and married me to my cousin. "Go, my son; there's no war there, and there's wealth, go." I left. I left the village near Marnia. We'll go there someday, we'll go there, you'll see, the country is beautiful.' My father has the hands of a farmer and a worker; they are rough and soft, I don't know how to explain it . . . We used to go to 'the island.' It's Seguin Island; you know it. The factory is on the island. It's closed now. They are going to demolish it; for what purpose? I don't know. My father doesn't want to hear about it. They would walk on the island, in my father's factory. His friends would hug me, swooping me up in their arms. 'Your dad is the best worker;

he's a leader . . . He's a skilled worker, but he's also a leader.' My father laughed; I think he loved me and I loved him too. Later, I learned why he was a leader. One day he said to me: 'The factory on the island is finished.' He wouldn't tell me why. I cried. I begged. I moped. I wouldn't kiss him, neither in the morning nor at night. He never gave in . . . I knew he had become a leader; he wasn't the workshop leader like my husband today . . . My father was a network leader of the group that organized the demonstration on October 17, 1961, at the factory and in the shantytown. I didn't know anything about it then. My mother did. I did think though that the adults, our parents, weren't speaking the same way they did before; they would change the topic of conversation or stop talking whenever I came into the room, the bedroom, up until the day when . . . But I didn't understand it all that day . . ."

Amel's mother stopped speaking. Archival photos of La Folie in Nanterre appear on the screen.

October 1961
The Owner of the Atlas Café

Inside, daytime

We went to school barefoot, in the snow, in winter . . . So, the mud in the shantytown doesn't scare me. My father died in the mud of the rice paddies in Indochina; his pension disappeared with him and his unit. I work for my mother, not for the clan. I don't have my elementary school certificate, but I know how to count. I run this café in this shitty place, but it does OK. I can't complain. I'll leave La Folie. I'll have a café at a city corner, a solid structure with a second story, a waitress, tables, chairs, a sturdy orange formica counter. I'll send money to my mother, if she isn't dead by then. Let my brothers and sisters fend for themselves, like me.

The "blue caps," Papon's *harkis*,[4] came several times. I don't know why they are called by that name. I'm not political. The others came too, the FLN.[5] They call me "brother," but they're not my brothers. I don't talk. "No alcohol, no tobacco. It is forbidden to play cards, to bet on the horses. If you disobey, you know what's coming to you." One of them lifted his head and put his finger on his throat, motioning from left to right. I understood. They also said: "There is an order from Headquarters, all businesses close on October 17, 1961." I don't have iron bars; I locked my wooden door with its key.

Nanterre. Amel and Omer

They are seated on a park bench in Nanterre. Omer is leafing through an Algerian newspaper. Amel takes off her dark glasses, looks at him; he continues reading. Amel strikes the paper with the back of her hand: "Is this the page about the massacres? Do you read that page every day? . . . You can't do without it . . . Read aloud so I can follow, as if I had a map in front of my eyes: Tlemcen, Aïn Defla, Médéa, Tiaret, Aflou, Blida, Algiers . . . Tizi-Ouzou . . ." "Have you been to Algeria? Do you know the country?" "No. My father says we'll be going there soon. I have a map of Algeria in my room. I stick in red pins to mark the massacres . . ." "Why?" "To know about them." "And what else do you learn from the pins?" "I'm learning terrorist geography." "And you believe you understand more that way, that you understand who is doing the killing, and the reason why? Just by placing a needle on the names?" "Is it enough to read the description of daily massacres, the way you do?" "You don't know what I read and yet you're talking about it; you don't know what I did or didn't do, or why I am in this country . . ." "This country is France." "I know, I know . . . You know nothing and you talk as if you did . . ." "You say nothing. You don't want to say a word." "Not now. We're looking for your shantytown without a clue, without a signpost, just like that, blindly. Go to city hall, check the land register, the map of the city in the 1960s. Go today; get information that will be useful to you. You're wasting your time. You don't know how to operate. You'll never be a journalist." "But I don't want to be a journalist, I definitely do not." "Why not?" "They are all fakes." "You don't know what you're talking about. Do you know what you want?" "Yes. My world is the theatre. I can recite Sophocles to you in Greek." "I don't believe you, and I wouldn't understand anything you say so don't bother. Why don't you come here with your mother? She must know where it is, or your grandmother?" "They don't want to. Every time I ask, they say: 'You'll find out when the time is right.'"

Amel hears her mother's voice.

The Mother

"My mother was the neighborhood dressmaker. She had learned the skill in her village. It was called Nemours. Today the name has changed; it's Ghazaouet, a port near the Moroccan border. My mother never bathed in the sea. Once, we went to the sea with my father, to a beach in Normandy, one of the D-Day beaches. I didn't like it. Neither did my mother. She said she never wanted to see the sea again. In Ghazaouet, she attended a sewing workshop, after school. Her father said: 'You know how to read, write, and sew. That's enough. Now you will stay home.' How did she meet my father? How did they get married? I don't know. My mother came to Nanterre. My father bought her a secondhand Singer sewing machine and she did dressmaking at home. Not only dressmaking. Working with women of the shantytown, she hid political tracts in fabric, in wedding dresses; the women distributed them. Women musicians would spread the news from wedding to wedding, from one celebration to another. I watched my mother and her friends prepare them; they said they were kitchen recipes and letters for the families back home . . . I later learned that the tracts were signed by the FLN. They were calling for the protest march on October 17, 1961. It was to be a peaceful march protesting the curfew imposed only on Algerians by the Paris prefect, Papon . . . He is the one they've been talking about; he'll be tried for having sent Jews to the Nazi camps. There has been a lot of talk about him; that's the same guy.

One morning, on a day in October, we heard screams coming from the little square, around a water station we called the fountain . . . When I saw water fountains in Paris . . . I knew that our fountain . . ." The mother stopped speaking and laughed; she repeats "our fountain . . . I still call it our fountain." Her face grows grave, like her dark eyes, and her beautiful mouth crumples. Louis hasn't moved the camera. The eye of the camera remains fixed on the mother.

"One October morning, women's shrill cries woke us up. My father couldn't stop us from going outside. In front of the door of the café that my father's brother ran, we saw a bloody corpse, its face in the mud, its arms stretched out, and near the body, a message from the FLN written in capital letters. My aunt was on her knees, her hair disheveled; she was screaming with other women, my cousins. My mother ran to them, forgetting me. I looked; it was my uncle. I recognized his red fez. He never took it off. I stood there for a long time, surrounded by the women's sobs and the men's hushed discussions. Blood had spilled into a muddy hollow; it was brown and red. I stared at it so I wouldn't have to look at the cadaver riddled with bullets. Did my father know that his brother belonged to the MNA,[6] a rival party of the FLN? He didn't answer my questions. I was already at the University, studying English at Nanterre. I wanted to visit American Indians . . .

When I was little, I read my brothers' cowboy and Indian comic strips . . . But that's not the reason. I wanted to live on the reservations with the Indians. I met my children's father, he was from Marnia, like my father . . . a mere chance . . . He too worked in 'the island' when he was very young and they were militants together . . . a mere chance . . . I was a student and my father refused to talk to me about the conflicts between the FLN and the MNA, his role and his brother's in these events, his brother's assassination, his body left for all to see, to serve as an example . . . Today others are carrying out assassinations, leaving cadavers to rot in public places, at the side of the road—the bodies of brothers, fathers, friends . . . enemies." A silence . . . a long silence that Louis did not cut.

The mother continues:

"That October day, for the first time I noticed that there were other men in uniform, not French, neither the French police nor the French army. I was a small child. I was nine years old, but I knew the difference. These men in uniform, under French command, looked like my father and like men in the shantytowns. They were Algerians and they were there, but not as brothers. My father told me: 'These men are our enemies. They're watching us; they're reporting us to the police; they're killing us. Beware of them; never talk to them. But, if you see one, move away; they are the plague, do you understand, the plague. They are called "Papon's harkis," "blue caps," collaborators . . . they're worse than the French police.' I'd see them in the streets of Paris. I was scared."

The mother stops speaking. There is a street; it's at night. Archival photos of men in uniform hitting other men, Algerian civilians.

October 1961
Papon's Harki

Outside, daytime

I was in the countryside. I was helping my uncle sell his wares at the market. He gave me vegetables and fruit for my family. I barely knew my father. He too had crossed the sea to earn a living. When I was born, he was in France. He sent money back to his brother for my mother. The first few years, he did, but then nothing more. We didn't know if he was sick or in the hospital, or dead, or if he had married a French woman . . . To this day I know nothing more. My uncle contributed to the FLN on our behalf; that worked out fine. French soldiers occupied the village. The SAS[7] officers would come to talk to us, coming into our courtyards. They would say, "In France you will have work, a salary, not like here . . . You are young; you will have a future there . . ." They would give us examples of Algerians who were like us, young, out of work. Over there, they had made it. "In France, there is no war, your life will be peaceful." My mother hesitated; she spoke with my uncle and with the French officer. She told me to take the chance. I left.

At Fort Noisy-le-Sec, near Romainville, I met up with Algerians from the countryside like myself. They had nothing to lose. We were promised the salary of a French police officer, with bonuses . . . We weren't going to say no . . . I knew how to read and write. They taught us to use weapons, handle an interrogation. The officer at Noisy found that I learned quickly and well. It's true that I liked it. I had a French policeman's uniform and a blue army cap. The officer looked at me the first day: "We don't recognize you, you're not the same guy, you are made for this uniform; you are great . . . You'll have all the women, that's for sure." It's true I wasn't sure I was still me. From that day on, everything changed. I aimed at perfection. They were happy with me. I was promoted. I got to know the Paris *medina* by heart. As for the FLN networks, I helped destroy more than one. I live in a hotel on Rue Château-des-Rentier, in the thirteenth arrondissement in Paris. I have cousins, *harki*s like myself, on Boulevard de la Gare and in hotels in the Goutte d'Or quarter. We meet in the Barbès cafés. We "make the cellars sing" as the Parisians say. As for the *méchoui,* our roasted lamb feasts, we had the best. I was picked with some others for surveillance in the Nanterre shantytowns and for night raids on FLN supporters. We would break everything in their shacks. On October 17, 1961, we blocked the Neuilly bridge, and on the 18th, we surrounded the Nanterre shantytowns; they were caught like rats.

We fired on demonstrators.

We threw demonstrators into the Seine.

Flora

Flora picks up the phone. It's Lalla. She's not crying, but she's about to, out of anger and sorrow. Amel, her favorite grandchild, has disappeared, without a word. And Lalla believed her granddaughter confided everything in her . . . well, almost everything.

Louis

Louis is writing a letter to Amel. He hasn't seen her since the film. Neither has Flora. He won't call Noria. They were going to go to Egypt together, he and Amel. At the age of ten, he had accompanied his father; he worked with Egyptian workers, and learned a few words of Arabic. They lived in the desert, under a tent, and at night, they slept under mosquito netting. He wants to film the traces of Bonaparte's scientific expedition and modern Egypt.

In his letter, he offers Amel a trip to the Orient.

Défense. Amel and Omer

They cross the Défense esplanade. Omer walks quickly. What is he going to say? That he's a correspondent for an Algerian paper in Paris . . . He doesn't feel like repeating the news reports that Algerians get. He can't carry out the investigation that interests him—the Kelkal affair—either in Islamic fundamentalist circles or by investigating the French secret service. He doesn't have the papers of a political refugee. Every day his mother tells him to take care of the formalities, but he doesn't do it. He'll go back to Algeria. Amel is dragging him across this esplanade. He knows what she's looking for but doesn't feel like helping her. He's tagging along because he has nothing better to do, like young Algerians who stand around "holding up the walls" in Algeria. In Paris, he has become a "Hittiste."[8] Amel takes him by the arm, makes him stop. "Did you know that from the obelisk at the Place de la Concorde you can see the Défense arch?" "No. So what?" "Well . . . if you had really watched Louis's film, you would know that at Défense, the Défense traffic circle, Neuilly bridge, Place de la Concorde, French police and Papon's harkis rounded up, beat, and killed Algerians on October 17, 1961. Didn't you see it? Did you know that already? You're not interested. Why not?"

Amel looks at Omer, surprised. She has taken off her dark glasses, her dark trench coat. "Watch it, someone is going to recognize you . . . If you belong to a clandestine commando group, be careful. And if I wind up at the police station because of you . . . I am letting you pursue your sentimental inquiry . . . ," Omer says as he approaches Amel. "Is this a threat?" "Yes, it is. Threats, I know all about them. A letter in Arabic signed by some GIA[9] group, a bar of black soap and a piece of cloth for my shroud . . . I received several of them . . . Until the day when I was riding in a car belonging to the newspaper, and they shot at me. They missed me, but the chauffeur, who was a friend of mine, was mortally wounded. So, threats, I know all about them . . ." "Who did it?" "I never found out. I left before I could find out; it was the third attempt on my life . . ."

They sit down at the Café de France. The statue of Marianne is visible in the distance. Amel fingers a curl, looks at Marianne, but says nothing. "Are you pouting? Oh, those temperamental women . . ." "No, no. I'm just not speaking, that's all." "Is it because the Algerians of October 1961 don't get me all worked up? Is that it?" "Maybe. I don't understand why you don't want to know about it. You know nothing about that day and those that followed, about that episode of the war. You know nothing about it and you don't want to know anything. It isn't important to you. Is it because today Algerians are killing Algerians? No one knows who or why . . . because your tragedy is more dramatic than my mother's and my grandmother's? Is that why?" "The history of the war of liberation, the official Algerian history, I know all that by heart, and it nauseates me. Do you understand?" "But that's not the official history. Louis's film, the archives, the eyewitness accounts . . . I knew nothing about it, nothing at all . . ." "If you'd like, someday I'll show you photos and texts I published in the Algerian press of Algerian women in the war; we didn't hear about them either here or there. You'll see the young sixteen-year-old girl and her mother, a schoolteacher from Tlemcen. You'll hear them speaking . . . without the image, without the sound. I think Louis's mother, Flora, knows them. You'll recognize my mother . . . You see, I'm not only interested in my own tragedy, as you say."

Amel gets up, walks towards the statue of Marianne. A giant woman, standing, as if she were poised to face the enemy, courageous. She is holding a flag, the banner of victory? Defeat? On one side, a long sword in its sheath, and in her right hand, a naked sword. She is leaning on a canon. A young man is seated at her feet, with a long rifle across his thighs. Amel reads the plaque to Omer who is not listening. She reads quickly, skipping words and names . . .

The statue
THE DEFENSE OF PARIS
inaugurated . . .
to recall the courage of the Parisians
during the terrible siege of 1870–1871.
Reinstalled at its original site . . .
It was inaugurated September 21, 1983 . . .

Omer interrupts her: "Why are you reading me this?" "First, because Parisians, the people of Paris resisted the enemy. Have you heard of the Paris Commune? And, because the statue was the spot where Algerians assembled for the march on October 17, 1961. Who defended them when the police charged on the Neuilly bridge? You heard the reports, the panic, bodies trampled, the wounded, the dead . . . Families dressed in their Sunday best, baby carriages turned upside down, lost shoes of adults, children . . ." "You would make an excellent history teacher, holding your students spellbound . . ." says Omer. He laughs because Amel turns her back on him. "Are you still pouting? Oh, no . . . I know, I know you'll be an actress like Isabelle Adjani. Why not? She hasn't played Sophocles in Greek, but if you're going to Greece, perhaps someone will write a play for you. Isn't that possible?" "Yes. I know that some day someone will write a play for me but not in Ancient Greek."

They approach the merry-go-round.

In a rococo moon, pink and blue, a mother and daughter go by. The young woman is dressed in *hijab;* she wears the Islamic scarf.

Amel hears her mother's voice.

The Mother

"My mother knew. Me, I thought we were going on a family walk. In the summer it was so hot in the shacks that my father—he used to buy the lamb for *Aïd*[10] at a farm in Normandy that belonged to a friend of his from the factory . . . Even today, our *Aïd* lamb is Norman—My father would say to us: 'We're going to the farm. Henri is coming to get us. Get ready. You have to be well-dressed and well-behaved.' Twice a year, until my father's friend passed away, we would go to the farm, in the truck; we kids were seated in the back, on the wooden benches. We loved Normandy, the meadows, the trees. There were no trees in the shantytown. There was just one lone tree that a peasant had planted. He was a Kabyle who wanted a tree for himself, in the mud of Nanterre. When the shantytown was being destroyed, he was there, to defend his tree. It wasn't cut down. It remained standing. At 7 Rue de la Fontaine, everyone was crying. We didn't want to be there, among the planks and the tin roofs. My father told us: 'If you wish, you can go to live with a family in the country. I know several and so does Henri. They take in foster children. They can ask for you.' We said no, and I hid in the flowered pleats of my mother's skirt.

That day, I think it was a Tuesday, I saw my mother searching through the suitcases. She put the linens in the suitcases, as if we were going on a trip. The suitcases were always full. We had two rooms with neither an armoire nor a closet; I never saw the old family trunk. My mother spoke about it every time she had to dress us up in our Sunday clothes. The tub was ready for the children's bath. Between the planks that served as an inner courtyard, my mother washed us, me first, because I was the youngest, then my brothers. We dressed up in our best clothes. My father said to me: 'You are always the prettiest, my daughter.' I was proud. He would take me by the hand and we would walk in the city. He told my mother: 'You go with the little one, and I'll take the boys. You're not in any danger. You know that . . .' I didn't understand why we were going separately and why we might be afraid. He added: 'it's peaceful'; several times he repeated 'peaceful.' I didn't know why he used that word, and said it three times. On the blue part of the world map I had read: PACIFIC.[11] I didn't ask any questions. My father was in a serious mood, preoccupied. We were not going to take our usual walk at the end of the day; it was weird. My brothers didn't say anything. They held each other's hands, staying close to my father. His moustache seemed darker and thicker, I thought. He had put on a tie, a lovely shirt, a velvet jacket. I said to him: 'Why don't you always dress like this?' He didn't answer. Maybe he didn't hear me.

We took the bus. My mother held my hand tightly. The neighbors weren't chatting the way they usually did. We were all together. We were silent. Défense, Étoile. The bus driver stopped. That's when I got scared. Police officers made men get off the bus, but not all of them, only those who looked Algerian. I saw men standing with their hands in the air, next to the bus. The police had billy clubs. I looked at my mother. She smiled at me. Her hand was warm. I didn't cry. I had never seen Paris. Here was Paris, and I saw nothing of it. Only men who looked like my father, with their hands on their heads. The French police and the other policemen wearing blue caps were stopping people coming out of the metro. They made them get into busses. Some were hitting those who weren't moving quickly enough. My mother's hand was warm, and a little clammy. She didn't speak. The other women didn't either. They got off the bus, we did too, and they said to the bus driver and the police: 'We're going home with our children.' This wasn't true. I heard my mother say to her neighbor: 'République.' Why République? In school, I learned about 'la république'—the republic—in history class. But here it was a password . . . That's what I thought.

Later, my mother told my father and her French friend, the woman doctor who used to come to the shantytown, she became a friend, you know; it was Flora, your mother. She said that from her seat in the bus, that evening, she saw, at a distance—the police weren't paying any attention to them— a man, a Frenchman, tall and thin, who was holding a young Algerian by the arm, as if he knew him; he walked a ways with him, far enough to make sure he wouldn't be picked up by the cops. My mother said she was sure the Frenchman had wanted to save the young Algerian. Perhaps she was right . . ."

Silence. The statue of Marianne on the Place de la République and the Tati department stores appear.

Once again the face of Amel's mother appears: "I forgot to say it was raining that evening."

October 1961
The Algerian Rescued from the Water

Outside, nighttime

It was October 17, 1961. It was raining.

I thought I was going to die. I was swallowing water from the Seine. I felt heavy, very heavy. I prayed. I had forgotten about praying. With work, you don't have time, you go to the café, drink a little; when rounds are served, it makes you drink. I didn't drink too much, but I did drink, and that's forbidden for us Muslims. I drank and the prayer . . . That night, the rain, the beatings, the cold water. The Seine smelled bad. The prayer came back to me. I prayed; I prayed . . . and I was saved. Otherwise, I would have drowned like the others. Their bodies were found carried away by the Seine. Surely, the Seine was red that day; at night you couldn't tell. When Algerians were pulled from the water, their hands and feet were tied. It took time to do that. I don't understand. They were dragged away, tied up, and after several blows to the head, tossed into the Seine? Or were there three bullets?

The Seine spit them back out. Even the Seine didn't want Algerians. How many? Maybe someday we'll know. And it seems that some were found strung up in the woods near Paris . . . And what about those killed during the peaceful demonstration? I know it was peaceful. No knives, no sticks, no weapons; those were the orders of the French Federation of the FLN.[12] I know. They marched with their families—wives and children, even elderly women—and they shouted and chanted the national anthem. They were clapping. The men did not defend themselves, they did not respond with violence. They obeyed the orders of the FLN.

And me, I found myself alone, I don't know how, with two cops and a "blue cap." They had nightsticks and billy clubs. I fainted from the blows. The cold water revived me. I don't know how to swim. I'm from the mountains. I came here as a child, but even so, I don't like the sea; I don't like water. I prayed so hard I didn't see my compatriots coming towards the Seine for me. They saved me. A Frenchman brought me to the hospital. I told my story. I don't know if the doctor believed me. I would like to have him testify, if some day . . .

I was dressed up that day. I wore a tie and everything.

République. Amel and Omer

Amel leaves the store with a large Tati shopping bag. Omer who was waiting for her at an outdoor café looks at her, smiling. "Why are you making fun of me? You would surely like to have some of them where you're from . . ." "Where I'm from?" "Yes, in Algiers, Oran, Constantine. With everything Algerians buy at Tati department stores . . . It's not expensive to shop there . . ." "Do you think we need this where I'm from? Is it crucial to have Tati?" "You're alive, aren't you?" Amel shows him the pink and white squares: "That's Brigitte Bardot's checkered cloth . . . You know that?" "I wasn't born yet. She's old, your BB, and stupid." "I wasn't born yet either. I don't give a damn about BB. My mother used to wear dresses in red and white checkered cloth, and my grandma Lalla also. It was inexpensive fabric and Lalla had her Singer sewing machine; she still has it at home. I saw photos of Lalla and my mother, wearing almost the identical dress, the same fabric . . . It's funny. I wouldn't have liked to dress like my mother . . . Did you know that BB said that we are barbarians because we slit the throats of lambs for *hallal* meat?[13] Jews do too, but she says nothing bad about them. She only criticizes Muslims. And lambs for *Aïd* . . . she doesn't want us to celebrate *Aïd*. She isn't the only one to say that and to think that if Muslims slit each other's throats . . . well, it's in the genes. You aren't saying anything. You're letting me talk on and on. Don't you have an opinion?" "If I told you what I thought you would be shocked. I don't want to shock you. Do you know the story of Abraham? Abraham and Isaac, Abraham and Ishmaël?" "No. But I don't see what would shock me." "Abraham agreed to the sacrifice because of his love for his God. He would have sacrificed Isaac, Ishmaël . . . Maybe he did and no one knew it. Since then, we sacrifice a lamb for *Aïd*, and boys are circumcised . . . The sacred legend tells us so. Legends are told to be believed, and we believe them. The truth . . . You know that Abraham sent away his servant Agar and his son Ishmaël at Sarah's command; she was Isaac's mother. Agar, alone in the desert, sent into exile . . . this was her *hijra*[14] . . . , received God's protection; he saved Agar and her son from death; in the desert, a spring burst forth; it is called *Zem-Zem*, its water is sacred, it cures all ills . . . My grandmother, who made the pilgrimage to Mecca, told me about it; she brought back some water . . . My mother never threw it away . . ." Amel interrupts Omer abruptly: "Why are you telling me this? Is it a lecture?" "If you want to think of it as a lecture, yes, so that you'll understand the rest, those of us who slit throats. They don't put a lamb or a doe in place of a human being. They think their act is sacred because they believe they are replicating the ancient act of submission to God. This act is proof of their absolute love for God. They carry the rite of purification to its extreme, by sacrificing women, men, children . . . They believe that the human body, like the sacrificial lamb, must by emptied of its blood. They believe the soul is in the blood, and that they are destroying all bad souls who are unworthy of God. You understand why; it is an act so ancient that it has become almost natural, each time it accompanies the concept of purification. You might not know this, but the *mujahidin*[15] didn't only slit enemy throats, French soldiers during the war, they also killed Algerian brothers they considered traitors. There were traitors, it's true, but I later learned, by reading books other than the official textbooks, and by listening to witnesses who spoke about those years of war against France, that often our militant brothers were executed by bullets or knives just like the fanatics who are killing their own people today and claim to be carrying out God's justice. Yes, I tell you, the act of slitting throats is within us. Do you understand?" "No. We are not murderers; I don't understand. Muslim revolutionaries are not all murderers . . . I don't understand what you mean." Amel clenches her fists under the table; she doesn't want to cry in front of Omer. Omer doesn't answer immediately. Amel calms down. He makes her put her hands on the round wooden table: "You have pretty hands. When I put them in mine, see how small they are." Amel pulls her hands back briskly, and turns toward the statue of Marianne, on the Place de la République. Omer says: "We have to live with that, you understand, with this act of death, the knife. Not only do we have to live with it, but we have to think about it, so that some day things will change. Do you understand?" "No." "Don't you want to understand?" "No." "Why do you always say no . . ."

They get up and walk to the foot of the statue, a giant sized woman in a toga with the laurels of victory and the tablets of Republican law, the Rights of Man. Three other giant women are seated at her feet, one holding a flag, another carrying a torch, the third—seated between Latin inscriptions engraved in stone that read PAX, LABOR—displays the fruits of the fertile earth in the folds of her robe. At her right there are wheat stalks, a bouquet of wildflowers, daisies, cornflowers, poppies, and at her left, two naked children are playing. "Another Marianne! You do like women in stone dressed as warriors for peace . . . It's weird . . ." says Omer. "We see her in Louis's film. Don't you remember?" Omer interrupts her: "So, now for you the truth is in Louis's film?" "It's the first time I saw or heard anything about October 17, 1961. Louis's film is the day my grandmother spoke about, 'when the time is right.' That's all. So, if you haven't forgotten, in the film we see photos, not many, and hear witnesses give their account of the march that went from République to the Grands Boulevards. Women, men and children . . . I would love to have seen Lalla and my mother . . . everyone in the parade shouting: 'Algeria for Algerians!' 'End the curfew!' 'Power to the FLN!' The women are clapping their hands, and ululating. It is raining. Where are the demonstrators heading? The CRS police push some of them back, but not all. Afterwards, it's total confusion; nobody seems to understand very well what is happening . . . You saw Louis's film, just like me. My mother spoke about République; she must have been there, with Lalla. I'll ask her. She can no longer tell me: 'Some other day.' She spoke to Louis, but said nothing to me . . ."

Before leaving République, they stopped in front of a merry-go-round, identical to the one at Défense. "It's a donkey from home," says Omer, pointing out the blue donkey on the merry-go-round, stopped in front of them. "They're blue?" "Yeah, our donkeys are blue."

They walk a long while until they reach the Grands Boulevards.

October 1961
The Owner of the
Goutte d'Or Café. Barbès

Interior, daytime

He was a good guy. I always called him: "Ali," I think his name was Ali, like many of my clients, I would always mix them up, all these years in the same bistro, first as a client, and now as the boss . . . I worked hard to get here. Nobody to boss me around . . . not even them, they don't boss me. They don't scare me, neither do the "blue caps." They don't trust me, I know, but they pay well for the evenings and the Algerian dancers. They come here for them. What they do with the girls after the café closes . . . I don't want to know. I do as I please, and the FLN orders don't scare me. Here, I'm the one who decides. They know it. They know who I am; they respect me. I have known the French police for a long time, long before the revolutionaries were born. I was born in this neighborhood. . . . forty-five years ago. They aren't going to teach me anything. My mother, my poor mother raised me the best she could, half of my childhood; she died young, and a girlfriend, also a prostitute, took care of me, out of pity. She taught me the profession, she taught me everything and today I'm in business for myself. I never knew my father, but from the only photo my mother left—it was in a large bag where she put everything she owned, taking it from hotel to hotel—he was an Algerian infantryman. I don't know Algeria. I'll never go there. My life is here. They don't like women over there, and not women like me . . . Women in the profession, I know all of them in this neighborhood. They come to my place, to rest, I give them drinks, they pay for them. There are no parasites, no unpaid bills in my bistro. I'm the one who collects the contributions, and there is never a cent missing, the "Brothers" can be sure of that. I'm the one who threatens the girls who don't want to chip in; even so, once a beating was called for, and it was a "Brother" who roughed up the "Rebel." That's what he called her and she never rebelled again. If I want to close up tonight, I will. If I don't want to, I won't. But I will close, because I won't have anybody. I may go to République, if it doesn't rain . . . Oops, I lost the thread of the conversation . . . I was speaking about the rug merchant, Ali. I was telling him: "Ali, why do you always wear a grey jacket? Do you want folks to think you are a schoolteacher?" He laughed. "I don't know how to read, I don't know how to write . . . I sell rugs, I don't want to get dirty." "Are they dirty? Didn't you say they are new? And your *chechia*?[16] You're the only Arab in the neighborhood with that thing on your head." "I'm fine like that." "People can tell right away that you're an Arab. In times like this, that's dangerous . . . " Clients at the counter would joke with Ali: "Is that a flying carpet or a stolen carpet?" "Buy my carpet, you'll go to paradise with the *houris* . . ."[17] I don't know who bought his rugs, I never knew. He paid his drinks, I never asked him anything, and he never told the story of his life.

I don't run an Arab café. I run a café-cabaret. The curfew from 8:30 PM to 5:30 AM didn't affect me. The police never threatened me, even though I had Arab clients and Arab whores. The police knew it, of course, but I had no trouble. Ali, the poor guy. He would come by, calmly. He wasn't suspicious enough of the cops. Three cops arrested him that day, October 17, 1961. They hit him, he was holding his stomach, they took him away, I never saw him again. If what happened to him was what happened to some others, from what I heard, they dumped him in the Seine.

Flora

The phone rings. Flora answers. No one. The phone rang several times during the day; on the other end, silence.

Louis

He often listened to his father's Egyptian friends with ardent discretion. He didn't understand everything, but when they spoke of Bonaparte's expedition of scholars and scientists, he could feel the anger in their voice. They would make wild gestures, get up, argue among themselves. He heard: "Colonial expedition," "manipulated scholars," "Bonaparte, the bloodthirsty conqueror," "the Oriental despot," "Bonaparte, inheritor of the Enlightenment." "Extraordinary statesman," "the modern Alexander the Great" . . . His father sided with the scholars, Berthollet, Geoffroy Saint-Hilaire, Monge . . . Louis heard the names of streets in the neighborhood where they lived, between the 13th and the 5th arrondissements. His father often spoke of Vivant Denon whom he admired. He was most likely a scholar.

When he decided he would go to Egypt to make a film with Amel, Louis spent entire days in the library of the Egyptology Society at the Collège de France. If it weren't for Egypt, he would never have had the idea of walking all the way down Rue Saint-Jacques to go to the Collège de France and read *La Description de l'Egypte* by the scholars of the 1798 expedition. For days and days—nights if he could—Louis lived in the library, dwelling in Egypt, with scholars, artists, Egyptians and Bonaparte . . . He no longer considers libraries to be for the old folks . . .

Flora

Flora picks up the phone. It's Noria. Her voice trembles: "Flora, I know you won't tell me anything, even if you've seen her, even if she spoke to you . . . I know. I'm not asking you anything, but tell me if you have seen her . . . If you know where she is. Tell me she is alive, Flora, tell me." "Amel is alive."

Louis

Amel hasn't answered his letter.

Louis continues to read the great books, dream about the illustrations, some colored, others not: animals, monuments, portraits and landscapes of modern Egypt. The turbans of the notables are works of art, the sketches of workshops, machines, mummies . . . Bonaparte's Egypt is not his father's. Why is he choosing to return to this country with Bonaparte and his scholars? He doesn't know why. Before leaving with Amel, he will go to see the photographs of 19th-century Egypt on display at the Institut du Monde Arabe, not far from the botanical gardens. He likes to stroll in the exotic hot houses and have tea at the Mosque in the little courtyard that is messy and somewhat dirty.

He reads Bonaparte's speech to his soldiers, who didn't yet know the goal of the expedition: "Soldiers: you are going to undertake a conquest with immeasurable effects upon civilization and world commerce . . . the first civilization that you will encounter was founded by Alexander." His father has friends who were born in Alexandria, Egyptian Jews who loved their city, their country, the Arabic language. He will go to see them, and speak to them, before his trip. He is learning Arabic.

Louis hasn't seen Amel. Flora hasn't either.

Place de la Concorde. Amel and Omer

They walk out of the metro. The stone façade of the station reads *métropolitain,* and on the pavement in front of the Hôtel de Crillon, they read the golden letters set against a black background. Two doormen, dressed in black and white uniforms, wearing black and gold caps, greet a foreign visitor. It's a palace. Place de la Concorde. "This is Concorde," says Amel, "and there's the obelisk and in front of us, Défense . . ." "I'm not a tourist and I don't care a damn about the obelisk. You sacked Egypt, first Bonaparte did, and you're proud . . ." "Stop carrying on as if I'm responsible . . . In any case, if it was Bonaparte, he did the right thing. The square is beautiful, it's all beautiful. . . . and this hotel. . . ." "Do you want to go in?" "Can we?" "Sure. Let's go."

Amel hears her mother.

The Mother

"I didn't tell you that my mother had combed my hair very carefully. She didn't use barrettes that time to tame my curls. The ribbons were ironed, just like the laundry she had taken out all creased from the suitcases. I told you about the suitcases. Flora saw them; she knows about them. She wore boots when she came to the shantytown. The ribbons, which I didn't recognize, were striped green and white. I wore two bows that I thought were too big when I caught a glimpse of them in the bus window. I told my mother I wanted to take them out. 'Oh no. Women, children, young girls, everyone has to wear green and white, our national colors.' I didn't ask for any further explanation; my mother seemed so serious . . . I lost a ribbon in the scuffle. We met Flora by chance, and she told us that Concorde was dangerous. The police were clubbing Algerians. The cops had machine guns. Her photographer friend showed her photos of the Concorde station, several weeks later. I saw them. On the metro platform, men,

Algerians, are being held with their hands on their head. It's
a roundup. They are going to be taken to detention centers
just like my father who was taken to the Palais des Sports
They are brought as far as a famous hotel, one I had never
seen. Flora told me the name of it; it sounds like 'Grillon.' Ask
her; the cops rounded up Algerians. We walked and walked
I didn't want to complain that my feet hurt. We were advised
to take the metro. The police were cordoning off the Grands
Boulevards, the public squares, the metro exits.

My mother walked toward a group of women who were
kneeling on the pavement. Flora said to her: 'Think of Noria,
she is still little, only nine years old . . . You shouldn't, Lalla
listen to me. Leave her with me. We will wait for you at
the foot of the tree, nearby. Believe me. I'm sure this is serious, these women on their knees.' My mother didn't listen
to Flora. She held me firmly by the hand. I was tired; we were
far from home; there wasn't even a bench to sit on, or a seat
in a café. They were all closed, well almost all, because of the
demonstration.

My mother walked up to the group of women. They were
crying silently around a body lying on the sidewalk, a young
man shot to death. She knelt down. I was beside her. Flora
remained at a distance. The women were praying and crying. For the first time, I heard my mother whisper verses of
the Koran . . . She prayed every day, alone, in the sewing
room. She waited for me to ask her to teach me. That's what
she told me when I said: 'I don't know the prayers.' I was
eleven years old. I began to pray with her from that moment
on. My mother stayed a long time with the women kneeling
on the pavement. Before she left, she gave one of them some
sheets of paper. I knew they were flyers for Women's Day, October 20. I knew what they were because she showed them to
me at Flora's, in the room where I slept that night. My mother

waited until morning for news of my father. She took the first metro to Nanterre. I stayed with Flora."

There are photos of Concorde station. On the platform, CONCORDE, in giant capital letters, white against a blue background, in a ceramic decorated frame. Police wearing caps are pushing Algerians against the white tiles. They have their hands on their heads.

In the next frame, we read: CONCORDE, white letters on a blue background without a frame. Around it there are blue letters on white tiles forming words. It's hard to read them. The camera zooms in on "forgotten," one letter in each little square, POWER, in disarray, LAW, DEFEND. "Place de la Concorde renovated, humanist, turn of the century . . ." says Louis's voice.

Omer and Amel enter the Crillon hotel. The two doormen follow them in. Omer says that he has reserved a room. The doormen accompany them to the front desk. Omer puts out his hand: "Room 7."

On the hotel cornice, you can see, if you look up, the statue of a woman, lying like an odalisque, surrounded by naked children, little Cupids. On each side of the cornice, there is an empty stone shield.

A hotel employee leaves the Concorde metro. He stands for a long time in front of the hotel façade. He reads red inked letters:

ON THIS SPOT ALGERIANS WERE SAVAGELY BEATEN
BY PREFECT PAPON'S POLICE ON OCTOBER 17 1961

October 1961
The French Lover

Inside, daytime

I found it on the morning of October 17, 1961, in the kitchen, near the blue coffee pot, in clear view. It was a political tract calling for Algerians to demonstrate on October 17, 1961. She never spoke to me about her political commitment nor about her activities in Paris. I thought she worked in a travel agency. That's what she said; that's what I believed. I was never sent to war because of my past history of tuberculosis.

I met her in Algeria, in a Roman city, at the seaside. She was interested in archeology, and I was too. The team had rented a Moorish house at the edge of the ruins. She was the first Algerian woman I knew who worked on Roman sites with men, and the youngest as well. We were all in love with her. I had a car, a sky blue Dauphine. I drove her to the Moroccan frontier, to a nondescript village, a small port, Port-Say, founded by a sugar magnate. I loved her. Love at first sight. I couldn't believe it. And she? I don't know. There was the war. We had to leave Tipasa, Cherchell and all the Algerian Roman ruins. I came back to Paris, before I left for Syria where I was sent on mission. I was sitting at an outdoor café, Place de la Sorbonne, in Paris. Was it the Sorbonne tobacco shop or Escholier? I wasn't paying attention. I was waiting for the next show at the cinema on Rue de Champollion. I wanted to see *Breathless*. I was reading the newspaper, *Le Monde*. I would always start with news of Algeria. It was during the war, but on that summer day in Paris, a person could be happy. Someone called me. I raised my head. There she was.

I didn't know that she had come to Paris to work in the resistance . . . She might have been setting bombs or gotten out of prison. She didn't tell me anything. I didn't ask her questions. She would have left me . . . That morning, October 17, she left without a word. I would have gone with her. I would have demonstrated with the Algerians. I thought she was alone, with neither friends nor family; she said she was forgetting Algeria . . . She lied to me. She'll never come back. If they learn of her affair with a Frenchman, if I'm not of interest to them, they will ask her—it will be an order—not to see me anymore. I looked for her, looking everywhere she might be, in all the places where people met. In Paris, I walked from the Neuilly bridge to Place de la République, searching in every direction. I witnessed scenes of violence against Algerians. I will testify. It was raining. It was night. I was hoping to find her in the kitchen the next morning, seated in front of a big blue and white checkered cup, her coffee cup. She wasn't there. She didn't show up the following days either. I went to the Arab cafés where I knew the FLN militants operated. I showed her photo. It wasn't a clever thing to do, I know. No one recognized her. Why would they have told me the truth? If they were protecting her, they wouldn't say anything and if she didn't belong to the network, they couldn't talk either. I believe I put her in danger without thinking. I waited. No one spoke of a woman drowned in the Seine, disappeared . . . Not at that time. Perhaps there were some, I don't know.

I went to the Algerian women's demonstration on October 20. I would have recognized her. She wasn't there. I thought she left the tract to trick me, that she had gone back to Algeria, that I would never see her again. What if she joined a group of terrorists? What if she had gone into the resistance? Some women did that. And then, one evening, just before I left for Syria, there she was, back at my home. I didn't ask any questions. I didn't say that I had been looking for her. I said nothing.

The next day, I left for Syria, with her.

Louis

Louis calls his mother: "Has Amel called? Have you seen her? Do you know where she is? And her family . . . she has a family after all and we know them. Have you spoken with Noria or Lalla? And her father, shouldn't he do something?" Flora becomes impatient: "Are you telling me what I should do? Amel disappeared. No news. Noria and Lalla don't telephone, and I don't call them either. That's all I can say, nothing else." Silence, and then Louis asks: "And Omer?" "What? Omer. He's an adult; he does what he wants to. Mina isn't worried. What do you want to know?" "Doesn't he live with his mother at your house?" "Yes, he does, but I don't spy on him, nor does his mother. He is twenty-seven years old. He knows what he's doing, even if he doesn't have his papers . . . He's going through the process . . ." "Does he go to the *préfecture* for his papers at night as well?" "But Louis, who is asking you to keep tabs on Omer?" "It's to protect him . . . And I want to talk to him, that's all . . . Do you think he is with Amel? Maybe they are wandering around Paris, just like that, carefree, and we're fretting." "Louis, you're speaking as if . . ." Louis hangs up.

In the Collège de France library, Louis writes to Amel. It's the second letter. He doesn't tell her he loves her. He writes to her about Egypt in 1798, the Orient that Europe dreams of conquering, discovering it to civilize, instruct, and occupy it. The cruel colonial myth. Finishing the letter, he tells himself that Amel will not read it to the end. He wrote her a history lecture. This isn't the letter he wants to write. A love letter . . . He doesn't know how. He rips the two pages into tiny pieces he saves at the bottom of his shirt pocket. He goes back to the description of Egypt, picking out sentences that amuse him. Geoffroy Saint-Hilaire writes to his friend Cuvier, in Novembre 1799: "The poor scholars working on Cairo were brought to Egypt so that we may read, in Bonaparte's history, yet another sentence of praise . . ." He wanted to tell Amel the story of the giraffe. There was a young giraffe from the Sudan that was treated like a human being. In 1826, Mohammed Ali, who was governing Egypt at the time, gave this famous giraffe to Charles X, the king of France. Geoffroy Saint-Hilaire goes to fetch it in Marseille where it spent the winter. It is presented to the royal family before being taken to the Museum menagerie. It's a great popular success . . . Will this giraffe touch Amel in the way it has touched him? He doubts it. He won't tell her about it in the letter.

He stops reading. He no longer takes notes. In the stillness of the library, and the shadows at the end of the day, he hasn't turn on the work lamp. He writes to Amel: "Amel, I love you. Let's go to Egypt, tomorrow, if you wish. Louis."

Bonne Nouvelle. Amel and Omer

They leave the Bonne Nouvelle station, cross the boulevard, enter the corner café.

They order coffee at the counter of the Gymnase café, a double expresso for Omer, an espresso with a bit of cream for Amel. Omar leafs through *Le Parisien*, the stock newspaper of café counters in Paris. He is looking for Algeria. Everything is going well. No news. Today, no terrorists killed by the Ninjas[18] either in the Algerian countryside or in the cities, no villagers massacred. All clear. He stops at the page of Horoscope and Games. He reads out loud: "'Aries: Use your energy for useful activities and leave the rest aside. Someone is worrying about you. Don't be so withdrawn.'" He says: "That's my sign . . ." "And you believe that? You do?" "I don't believe it, but in this case, it's the truth. At least, in part. What's your sign? Sagittarius. Let me read it, it's important. You don't believe me? Good, let me read it: 'You can't be described as someone with a calm and peaceful nature. Right now, you are moving in all directions and don't know which way to turn.' So, is this true or not?" "It's somewhat true," Amel says, not knowing if Omer is joking or not. Leaving the metro at Strasbourg Saint-Denis, Amel took a card given to her by an African. She gives it to Omer; "If you believe in it, you will know everything, look: 'Mr. Kaba, great medium, great clairvoyant . . . authentic African *marabout* . . . Protection against your enemies . . . Don't hesitate to contact Mr. Kaba's office.' If you want his address, it is in the 18th arrondissement, Rue des Poissonniers. We are on Rue du Faubourg-Poissonnière, we're under the sign of the fish today. The fish is a lovely symbol; did you know that? On the radio, you can listen to the special programs devoted to clairvoyance. You'll have no more bad surprises . . ." Omer interrupts Amel: "In Algeria, fortune tellers are called witches; they are being persecuted by Islamic militants; several have had their throats slit. Islamists forbid alcohol, tobacco, gambling, music, newspapers, and fortune telling. For them, and for others as well, God is the sole master of the destiny of men, his creatures. Every individual who pretends to read the future must be punished. No freedom. Everything is predetermined. No choices in one's life. Maybe it's easier."

The café owner is a bosomy blond. She is about sixty-five years old. She handles the cash register, serves at the bar, chats with the clients. Amel asks her: "Were you already here thirty-five years ago? In 1961?" The café owner bursts out laughing: "Well . . . I was far, far away at that time, and I didn't think I'd have a bistro some day. We don't always do want we want to in life, you know . . . Me, I believe in fate. I came to France, to Marseille. I had nothing. In 1962, you must know, the Algerians chased us out. They sent us packing, taking everything, the villa, the business . . . we received compensation in tiny doses. I was young. I had no children.

My husband was a courageous man, thank God. He never took part in the dirty war. He managed to pull through, and we picked up a small business in Marseille, and then one in Paris. We weren't doing great, but it was OK. We bought the Gymnase Bistro ten years ago. My husband died; he was killed in a car accident three years ago. I didn't want to take on a manager. I prefer to be on the job . . . But, why are you asking me this question? 1961. What happened then? We were packing our bags over there. We knew we couldn't stay on. They didn't like us, and we didn't like them either. Of course, in a café, all clients are served and in Marseille, the Porte d'Aix neighborhood, where there were only Arabs, we served them. They never meant us any harm; after all, they weren't at home here either. Me, I've been French forever, but I had never been to France. My family was Maltese and Spanish. For me, France was far away. Now, I get along really well with Arabs. My cook is Arab. Isn't that true, Mourad?" An Algerian walks past the counter; he is a tall, thin, handsome man wearing a white jacket and apron; his hair is curly, salt and pepper. He dries his hands on his apron, goes towards the cash register, smiles at his boss. "Mourad, tell them we get along well, you, an Arab, me, a French woman. I pay you what I would pay a Frenchman. You eat at my table. You're a good worker . . . Maybe you were a waiter in 1961? You would have been very young at the time, of course. How old were you then? Sixteen? Seventeen? You weren't a waiter; you weren't of legal age. Were you in Paris in 1961?" The cook looks at his boss, then at Omer and Amel to whom he asks: "Were you the one asking about 1961?" "Yes, I wanted to know about October 17, 1961 and what happened on the boulevards, Bonne Nouvelle, Poissonnière, and on the sidewalk in front in the Rex cinema . . . You can see the Rex from here, and next to it the Quick fast food restaurant, and across the street, MacDonald's . . ." "Oh my . . . None of them existed in 1961. The Rex, yes, and the Gymnase, too, with the Gymnase Theater next to it. All of that was there, but the rest . . . I was young. I think I was 16 years old at the time. And I saw it all, well, everything . . . from where I was. I haven't forgotten any of it." He doesn't look at the café owner as he tells his story:

"I was with my uncle that day. He wasn't a militant but he wanted to take part in the march in Paris with the Algerians demanding an end to the curfew. He had witnessed the settling of old scores between the MNA and the FLN in his neighborhood. It had made him sick, and so that's when he decided that politics for him . . . instead of coming together, they kill one another . . . Well, it's the same today between the FFS[19] and the RCD.[20] Wouldn't you think they could come together so Algeria might change? The military, the police, they get stronger and stronger, so democracy in our homeland . . . We came in from Argenteuil, with others who worked in construction like us, a group of workers with their families. My uncle was a bachelor at the time. We had barely gotten out of the metro at Bonne Nouvelle when the cops—Papon's French and Arab police—stopped us. I learned later that the head of the Paris police was Papon, the same civil servant who signed the deportation order for the Jews arrested in the Gironde region, the same one sent on a special mission to Constantine during the Algerian war . . . I've read lots of books about the war. I was too young at the time, and I wanted to find out about it. I went to a library in my neighborhood. The director was married to an Algerian; she gave me books to read. Today, I'm a cook working for Madame Yvonne, but I could have worked in a library . . . I'm not going to tell you my life story . . . We left the metro to join the demonstration, and there were cops everywhere. I don't know why it went bad. None of us provoked anything. I'm a witness to that, no one. The men tried to protect the women and children. They took the blows; there was an indescribable melée. I lost track of my uncle. I ran to the Gymnase to protect myself, like others. I ran into the Rue du Faubourg-Poissonière. The police were in front of the Gymnase theater, the café, and the Rex cinema. I heard the cops say: 'They're like rats, they keep coming out . . . They are vermin. We have to destroy these rats. They think they're at home here. Just let them see if they can do what they want . . . And those sluts, those French women, what are they doing here with them? . . . Those sluts, they want to get laid by Arabs. I tell you, they are all sluts . . .' They were hitting the Arabs while insulting them. They were full of hatred. They thought their co-workers had been wounded; that's what the radio wanted them to believe. Lies. When I came back towards the boulevards, I didn't see any wounded cops either in the street or on the sidewalk. I saw my compatriots, several bodies stretched out in front of the Gymnase and the Rex. Algerians had bullet wounds, not just injuries from the beatings. And the folks looking down from the balcony of an apartment building were taking pictures. That was clear. I saw them at number 6, Poissonnière Boulevard. Journalists were there too. They can testify as well. There were hats, scarves, shoes scattered on the concrete. All of that was lost, abandoned in the panic. I wanted to testify, but there was never an occasion, and now, here I am at this bar talking about it to you, for the first time in thirty-five years. Over the years, I forgot. You have to work, and when you work, you forget. It was the Papon Affair that brought it all back. I didn't even speak about it with Madame Yvonne." The café owner listened to the cook until the end, without interrupting him. Clients were left waiting to be served. They stayed at the bar, attentive to Mourad's story. The café owner said: "And we folks, over there, we heard nothing about any of this. That's strange. How could that be?" Mourad murmurs: "Did you take an interest in the Algerians living in Paris, you, *pieds noirs?*"[21] "No, you're right. We didn't give a damn about Algerians in Paris. We already had enough Arabs to deal with. Those guys over there, they scared us, that's for sure." Mourad hands Amel a piece of paper: "Go see my uncle; here is his address. He still lives in Argenteuil. He is married; he has children your age . . . They will know about it too." The café owner says: "My goodness . . . I never heard about this. In any case, it's past history. You can't cry about it now . . . Hey, let me offer you whatever you'd like. What would you like?"

Amel drinks a Coke.

Omer has a pint of Leffe on tap.

October 30, 1961
The French Student

Inside, daytime

I was at the Solferino station that day, October 17, 1961. The French had not been invited to participate in the Paris demonstration by the Algerian organizers of the French Federation of the FLN. Out of solidarity, some would have been there. One of the directives of the resistance network was to observe, witness, but not participate directly. Photographer friends risked their lives, taking photos at Concorde, Solferino, the Neuilly bridge, Nanterre. One of them, a friend of my parents, Elie Kagan, went across Paris on his Vespa scooter to Nanterre where he knew Algerians had been killed. I saw very few photos of that tragic day. On the whole, journalists didn't do their job.

At Jean-Baptiste-Say high school, my friends and I in our senior class organized a strike protesting the Algerian war. We were not suspended. Our fathers were not workers at the Renault plant in Boulogne-Billancourt. They were engineers, production heads, business executives. The principal didn't dare punish us. I had a Kabyle friend. He came with me, one July 14th—Bastille Day—to distribute pages of the banned book *The Question* that Jerome Lindon had published with Éditions de Minuit. These kinds of tracts had been published, "good tracts," as they were called in the publishing world, to expose the fact that the military was practicing torture in Algeria. Henri Alleg dared write the book. I believe he was living in Algeria. This was in 1958 or 1959. I have already forgotten the dates . . . My memory is weak.

I knew about the demonstration scheduled for October 17, 1961. I had read the tracts put out by the FLN. My father had brought some home. I said that I would either go to Place de l'Étoile or Place de la République. My mother tried to dissuade me. Violence scares her, maybe because of the successive exodus of Ukrainian Jews . . . Her family left the Ukraine at the beginning of the century, to settle in France, like many Russians, Jews and non-Jews. My father said the march would be peaceful and familial.

When I arrived at Solferino, the station was deserted. A man was seated all alone on a bench. He had been wounded in the head. Blood was flowing from the wound. He was disoriented. I helped him. I took the metro with him. He didn't want to go to the hospital. He said it wasn't serious. I accompanied him to Argenteuil. He had worn his Sunday clothes, a tie, a vest under his suit jacket. His white shirt was spattered with blood.

At home, I turned on the radio. Everything was calm in Paris. It was as if nothing had happened. They were announcing Ray Charles's concert scheduled for October 20 at the Palais des Sports, in Paris. I listened to Ray Charles and I read *The Deserter* by Maurienne that I had bought at "Maspero's bookstore," that's what we called "La Joie de lire," the book shop on Rue Saint-Séverin owned by publisher François Maspéro. Like *The Question,* it was published by Éditions de Minuit. I don't know the name of the author who had deserted. I'll find out some day. The book tells the story of a young French conscript who refuses to fight the Algerian revolutionaries. He deserts.

Flora

Flora calls Nanterre.

No one is home at Noria's. No one at Lalla's. She calls
Louis. Since the day they watched the film together several
times, all three of them, he hasn't seen them, neither Amel
nor Omer. Mina is worried. There has been no news of her
son. It has been more than a week. She called Algiers. His father doesn't know anything.

Saint-Michel. Amel and Omer

They are chatting at the Saint-Michel fountain. Omer's shoulder is covering part of the inscription on the marble plaque, below the bronze griffin, spitting water. One can read an incomplete text:

IN MEMORY

OF THE SOLDIERS OF THE FRENCH FORCES

OF THE INTERIOR AND THE INHABITANTS OF THE VTH AND

ARRONDISSEMENTS WHICH ON THIS SITE

DEAD IN BATTLE

Perched on a rock, Saint Michael as a winged warrior, with his sword in hand, defeats the dragon, a man with a devil's head.

Louis filmed the fountain.

Amel hears her mother's voice.

The Mother

"I forgot to tell you . . . Louis, when you tell a story, you forget, everything comes back pell-mell. I can't quite recall the precise order of events that day. You will have to ask Lalla. You must put your film together chronologically, if you are able to do so, because I think the demonstration occurred simultaneously in several places. Flora will tell you what she knows . . . I had forgotten the famous Saint-Michel fountain. Before arriving on foot at Flora's . . . I was so frightened, and so was my mother, even if she didn't show it. I saw the fountain, and I already told you it was the first time I had seen Paris, but I didn't really see it that day. I did see the fountain; it made me think of our fountain in the shantytown, a tiny, ridiculous watering hole. I found this fountain to be majestic, even though I barely had time to look at it. The police charged . . . Later I saw the police charge the same way, but I wasn't there; it was May 1968 . . . I followed all of that on television. We were in a low-income housing project at

the time, after the transit housing project. We were watching the pictures on the news, with the family. My brothers
were there, too. May 1968 didn't concern us, the Arabs living in the projects . . . We didn't see many Arabs among the
university students. By then, my mother was doing less sewing at home; women were buying their clothes in department stores. It was cheaper for them than going to a dressmaker. This was true for them, and their children . . . I am
telling you all of this in case it has some interest for your film,
otherwise, don't hesitate to cut it. So, my mother found work
on the Nanterre university campus. She was head of a crew
working for a janitorial service. At that time we hadn't yet
begun to call janitorial staff 'surface technicians.' She was
at the campus on March 22, 1968 when Dany Cohn-Bendit
took over the administrative building with other students,
they called for a strike at Nanterre and the Sorbonne . . . Nanterre was occupied; my mother could no longer clean the
building. The Sorbonne was occupied and we saw the dem-
onstrations, the barricades, all of that was on TV. Students
jeered at the police, shouting 'CRS . . . SS . . .'[22] They chopped
down the plane trees on the Boulevard Saint-Michel. These
were the trees that had protected us, my mother and me,
from the blows of the cops' billy clubs. Maybe even from
the CRS, I can't remember. They struck blows in all directions. They pursued Algerians into the neighborhood streets,
la Huchette, Saint-Séverin, la Harpe. They took them away
in busses. For a moment, I thought I was lost. I had let go of
my mother's hand. I began to scream. I heard my mother
call my name. I didn't see her. Men were falling down, and
cops were beating them with billy clubs. Where did these
billy clubs come from? I later learned their name. It was my
mother who told me: 'In Algeria, we buy them in the market.' Are they for the animals? Do they get the donkeys to

move? Are they used to hit vagrants? I never knew. On that day, the police were armed with clubs, firearms, night sticks. Maybe the 'blue caps' brought them directly from Algeria? A firm hand grabbed mine. It was my mother. We ran to a bookstore. The door opened, just partway. We were pulled inside. My mother huddled with me, in the back, behind a pile of books. A young bookseller showed me to the bathroom. I was so scared . . ."

The camera stops a moment, films an empty store on Saint-Séverin, next to the Hotel Europe whose letters are etched in stone.

Empty bottles are floating on the water at the edge of the fountain: Coca-Cola, Schweppes, beer, and empty wrappers and food containers from MacDonald's. At the square, there are motorcycles and bikers dressed like members of the CRS. Amel and Omer walk towards the Rue de la Harpe, stopping at the Pâtisserie du Sud, the Tunisian pastry shop. They eat a cold, oily, too sugary, beignet. They take Rue Saint-Séverin. They don't see any bookstore. There are tourists, and Greek and Turkish restaurants, an odor of grilled lamb, grilled sausage. They reach Place de la Sorbonne via Rue Champollion and sit on the terrace of L'Escholier. Omer turns to Amel: "Do you think we can be unhappy, here, in this city, on this square, with these trees, at the end of this day, in Indian summer . . ." "And, of course, the queen of Sheba, . . . If there hadn't been *Aïsha,* the queen of Sheba, we wouldn't be happy . . . How can we live without Khaled[23] . . . Do you listen to him?" "I don't like that guy. No, I don't listen to him. He's a clown like the other one you all idolize, the old druggie, Johnny[24] . . ." "Again it's 'you all' . . . how long is that going to last? It's true that I have French papers, but I don't represent all the

French . . . I can like Khaled without liking Johnny. What do you have against Khaled? He's an international star; he takes French songs throughout the world . . . It's true . . ." "So the French are the buffoons, those who want to be represented by 'Y'a bon banania,'[25] the grinning minstrel smile. A product made for jerks . . . that's your Khaled." "Everyone loves him, me too. You're not going to stop me . . ." "You can like whomever you want but I'm not obliged to listen to that jerk and his queen of Sheba. That's exotic trash, and it's a crowd pleaser . . . You know what I think? Louis's film is going to be a flop . . . Who wants to listen to the story about that day, October 17, 1961? Who? Neither the French nor the Algerians, neither immigrants nor native-born nationals . . . So . . . All of that for nothing. They prefer Khaled and his nonsense . . . or Algeria destroying itself, Algeria bleeding, Algeria in the dark, in deep shit. After more than thirty years of independence . . . what sweet revenge . . . And it's Khaled who defends democracy, poor Khaled threatened by Islamic extremist monsters. It's ludicrous. That's what I say. Are you listening to me?" Amel makes noise with the straw in her Coke. "Are you listening to me? If it's another Khaled song, I'm leaving." "It's Etienne Daho. Do you know him?" "No, I've never heard of him. Is he good?" "I like him. Guess what? I learned he's the son of a *harki* . . . Imagine. Possibly, his father was a 'blue cap.' He always hid the fact that he is Algerian, well, French of Algerian parents, 'French Muslims' as *harki*s are called." "Who told you that? It might not be true." "Someone who knew his father, and in any case, I checked it out. Daho is an Algerian name and if you had seen him on TV, you would know he has the face of an Algerian. He couldn't hide that despite the fact that he looks like a dandy . . . Look, I'm glad that he's an Arab, and that he doesn't sing like an Arab. Do you understand?" "I understand, I do. I also understand that you are complicated. You're a little mixed up, aren't you?" "What do you mean mixed up? Is that an insult?" "Not really. I'm mixed up too."

Amel takes the last sip of Coke through her straw. Omer gets up.

Amel says: "Where are we going?"

Omer replies: "You'll see."

Several days later, on the quai at Saint-Michel, Louis films the red letters:

ON THIS SPOT ALGERIANS FELL
FOR THE INDEPENDENCE OF ALGERIA
OCTOBER 17, 1961

October 17, 1961
The Bookseller of Rue Saint-Séverin

Outside, nighttime

Friends had warned us. They knew that Algerians would be demonstrating with their families today in Paris. They said it was important, after everything that had happened recently: arrests in the shantytowns of the suburbs, raids in the Arab cafés, arbitrary arrests, detentions in camps, mobilization of the Paris police, CRS, mobile squads, "blue caps." A police chief who had sent Jews to their death . . . We also knew that the settling of scores by rival political factions was taking place in Algerian neighborhoods. François Maspéro did not want to close the bookstore—his bookstore, "La Joie de lire," on Rue Saint-Séverin—where militant revolutionaries, neighborhood students, intellectuals involved in political struggles, those supporting liberation wars, all came by. His clients call it "Maspéro's bookstore." It's like a literary and political salon. Everyone knows what's going on and everything that is important; that day, people thought Algerians were right to call for an end to the curfew. Books that couldn't be found in other bookstores, particularly banned books, those condemning the Algerian war, the massacres, the torture, those books were not on the shelves, but they were available to anyone who asked for them.

We told each other that because of the rain, the demonstration would not be successful. The organizers were anticipating thousands of Algerians from the suburbs coming with their wives and children. The cops cordoned off the neighborhood as if they were expecting a riot. Police vans were stationed around the Saint-Michel fountain, and in the neighboring streets. We heard the cops. They were speaking loudly: "What do those lousy Arabs think . . . They are not at home here. They come here looking for trouble. The street doesn't belong to them; neither does the city. France is not Algeria. They come with their *Fatmas* and their whole clan. They call for security forces of order. Security forces, that's us . . . We didn't get rid of enough of them, those *Fellouzes*[26] . . . If anyone had listened to me, there wouldn't be many more FLN left . . . Yeah, we'll see. We could have won Indochina, and we lost. We're not going to lose Algeria . . ."

I saw it, and I am not the only witness. There were my colleagues, and Maspéro as well. We all saw the unleashing of hatred and violence, the cruelty of some of the cops. They were using rifle butts, billy clubs, whips. They were hitting men, women, they didn't even spare the women. They were hitting old people. They beat up an old man. His turban was no protection. He was in the gutter, covered with blood. Some Algerians ran to the riverbank. The Seine is not far, just behind us. Some people threw themselves into the river; others fell over the side of the bridge . . . Panic. Surely at the Saint-Michel Bridge, the Seine was red. I didn't see the color. Along with Maspéro, we tended to the wounded in the bookstore.

and accompanied Algerians to the pharmacy. I don't know what happened in other parts of the city: République, Opéra, Étoile . . . the Grands Boulevards . . . We'll know tomorrow. It will be in the papers. But I saw bodies around the fountain, the wounded, and lost children crying . . . The owner of the Oriental cabaret, the Djezaïr, on Rue de la Huchette, helped us along with other Algerians and French people from the neighborhood. The police arrested hundreds of Algerians. They took them away in busses, but where did they go?

Louis

Louis calls Nanterre.

Noria answers: "Is it Louis? Did you see Amel? Her father is furious. If Amel isn't here, if we have no news by tomorrow, he is going to the police to file a missing persons report. We don't understand. Lalla cries all day long. She waits by the telephone, her little Amel . . . So, that's her little Amel. That's what she is doing to us . . . I don't understand. I don't understand anything . . . What about you, Louis?" "We watched the film together with Omer. You know, the suitcase couriers, the Algerian war, October 17, 1961. That was about a week ago. I don't remember exactly. Since then, no one's been around, neither Amel nor Omer." "Has she gone off with Omer? Do you think so?" "I don't know. Maybe it's the film that . . ." "Why the film? I don't see why . . . I'll call Flora. I want to know. And Mina, maybe she knows where the two of them, Amel and Omer, might be." "Call her, you'll see . . . If I see her, I'll let you know. Bye."

Orly. Amel and Omer

Orly Airport. Omer and Amel are drinking coffee at the cafeteria counter. Amel rips up drafts of letters. "I'll never be able to do it. They won't believe me. They'll think I'm crazy. They'll never understand. I don't want to explain . . . I'll tell them when I get back. Then we'll be able to talk it over. I'll say the day 'when the time was right' arrived. I lived through it, I learned the truth, not the whole truth. I'll say that day was not a day of woe as Lalla predicted . . . In the meantime, what do I write?" Amel sets herself to the task. She writes on the back of a postcard of La Défense:

"Everything is OK. See you soon. Your Amel."

Amel reads and rereads her airline ticket: "How did you do this?" "Well . . . that's my secret . . . Don't worry, everything is in order." Amel looks at the planes: "My grandfather was deported. He boarded the plane at Orly with other Algerians; it seems there were several hundred of them on October 19, 1961 . . ."

"I know," says Omer. "We will also be boarding the plane in a little while."

They hear her mother's voice.

The Mother

"My father wasn't at home. My brothers were. They had eluded the police thanks to my father's friends, French people who were not in the march but were on the sidewalk, observing. Flora will tell you about that. My mother waited all night. The next day, she went to see the organizers. Many people had been arrested. They told her that she would probably find her husband in one of the detention centers where the police were holding the Algerians they had arrested, more than ten thousand of them . . . They mentioned the Palais des Sports, the Sports Arena. I was at Flora's. I wanted to be with my mother, but she said no. I knew about the Palais des Sports. She spoke about it to Flora when I was there. I heard it all. Hundreds of men were jammed in, confined. They were beaten, bruised, clubbed . . . They had to empty their pockets in one place. There were billfolds, cigarette packs, matchboxes, combs, watches, handkerchiefs, metro tickets, bus tickets, chewing tobacco tins . . . There was a stack three feet high. No bathrooms . . . They stayed there until they were deported. My father was one of those deported.

They were taken to Orly. They couldn't contact anyone, neither relatives nor friends. On October 19, 1961 a load of Algerians considered 'undesirable on French soil' boarded two Air France planes, under the surveillance of the CRS. They went back to 'their home villages,' which were detention centers. My mother learned several days later, via Flora's friends, that my father was being held in a camp near Médéa, on a farm. He stayed there until the ceasefire. Meanwhile, the Palais des Sports was evacuated, and cleaned up for the Ray Charles concert scheduled for October 20, 1961. The concert took place.

On October 20, with Flora, my mother decided to participate in the Algerian women's rally, called by the French Federation of the FLN. Their slogans were 'Freedom for our husbands and children,' 'End the racist curfew,' 'Full independence for Algeria.' I was with them in Paris. We marched to Sainte-Anne Hospital. I didn't know it was a psychiatric hospital or why women and children were meeting there. Maybe because it was not far from La Santé prison where Algerian men were locked up . . . You will have to ask Flora or my mother about that. There were several hundred women and children. The police were armed. Nurses helped us. We escaped through the back door. This time I wasn't scared.

We learned later that Algerians had been killed. It was already known in Nanterre; there, we didn't have to wait for the official report. The River Patrol had brought up dozens of bodies. The exact number was never known.

We waited for my father. I didn't want to go back to school. I didn't want to leave my mother. We watched for the mailman. When my mother received the first letter, she said to me: 'Your father is well. He sends you hugs and kisses. He says that you must be good. He will be back soon.' I understood. The next day I went back to school."

October 1961
The Cop at Clichy

Outside, daytime

I am not the only one who witnessed it. Several of us did, not many, that's for sure, but some of us. On that day, October 17, 1961, the Algerians had not come to Paris to create havoc; it was a peaceful demonstration. They did not fire on us; they were not armed; maybe the security forces . . . Nothing was found on them when they were searched and their pockets emptied. I don't particularly like Arabs. In fact, I don't know much about them. I haven't been in Paris for very long. Before then, I was in Poitiers where you don't see Arabs. My youngest brother, the one who was supposed to work on the farm, was sent to Algeria. He writes letters home. He doesn't mention Arabs. He says everything is fine. He doesn't want to worry the old folks. So, we don't know much. I have been in Paris for two years now. I never worked with the "blue caps." It seems those guys are the worst; they're fierce. I have heard they work in the cellars, and they're not gentle, even though their prisoners are Muslims like themselves. They use what they call the "Méchoui method." I have never seen it, but my colleagues have told me about it. They attach the prisoner by his hands and feet to a stick, like a deer or a lamb. They spin him around hitting him with a whip or a billy club . . .

I never saw that, but I did see—I was there, I didn't dream this up, and there are other witnesses—I saw cops shoot Algerians and toss them over the bridge into the Seine. I saw this; there were several of them. I couldn't intervene. I was too far away, and it happened too quickly. Some cops have blood on their hands, that's for sure, and it's Algerian blood. I'm clear about that. I saw blood on the bridge parapet . . . It wasn't pig's blood . . . It was Arab's blood. At that spot, the Seine was red, I'm sure. Even though the visibility was poor and it was dark and rainy. I'm going to testify. I know I'm risking my job, and if I am demoted, I'll be sent back to Poitiers; so much the better. I'm prepared to testify as needed. I'm sure that these colleagues of mine served in Indochina or somewhere similar . . . In my opinion, that day, they disgraced the reputation of the Paris police. That's what I think and I'm not alone. The newspapers are going to report it, if they are honest.

October 17, 1961, is a dark day for the Paris police. We can call it Black October . . . because the River Patrol recovered Algerian bodies, and not only in Paris. How many? We'll know someday. Not just three or four, several dozen, I'm sure. We'll know. No other possibility. We'll know. In a few years, maybe ten, twenty, thirty . . . we'll know. Word always gets out.

Louis

Louis calls Flora. He doesn't talk about Amel. He says: "I'm leaving for Egypt. I'm taking the plane tomorrow morning. I don't know how long I'll stay there. I am going to see Dad. I know where he works. He went back to the place he brought me to fifteen years ago. I'll find it. I'm taking the novels about Alexandria, 'the quartet' . . . I know they are yours, and that you are attached to them. I'll be careful. Bye." He hangs up. Flora didn't have the chance to speak.

Alexandria. Amel and Omer. Louis

They are seated at an outdoor café, in Alexandria.

Someone calls to them from the other side of the street: "Omer! Amel! Omer! Amel!" They hear the call to prayer. Louis runs across the street:

"What are you doing here?" "You see, we're having coffee in Alexandria, and then we'll go up the Nile, to the end of the river. I'm writing a play for Amel. Not in Classical Greek." "What's it about?" "It's the story of a girl who digs a grave for her brothers at night, on a hill. She works hard at it; the ground is hard. Soldiers are guarding the bodies of her twin brothers; they were executed. The army displayed the bodies on the village square . . ." "It's sinister" says Louis.

"Yes, it is sinister . . . What about you, what are you doing here?" "I wanted to follow Bonaparte's scholars . . . Afterwards, I'm going to look for a site, in Egypt, in the Sinai, perhaps in Sudan . . . for a film." "And who is your heroine? Do you know yet?" "Yes, it's Amel . . ."

Notes

INTRODUCTION

1. For further historical perspectives, see Einaudi, Brooks and Hayling, Laronde.

2. For a further discussion of Sebbar's views concerning a life of exile, see *Lettres parisiennes*.

3. Letter from Leïla Sebbar to Mildred Mortimer, May 27, 2007.

4. First published in *Actualité de l'émigration hebdo*, no. 207 (1990), pp. 14–16; it reappeared in a later version in *Le Maghreb Littéraire*, II: 3 (1998), pp. 95–98.

5. For further study of *anamnesis* in Sebbar's work, see Donadey's articles.

6. During a visit to the United States in spring 2002, Leïla Sebbar visited Professor Michel Laronde's literature classes at the University of Iowa. She made this comment during class discussion. I thank Michel Laronde for sharing the video with me.

7. Sebbar, University of Iowa, 2002.

8. Ibid.

THE NOVEL

1. There is irony in the fact that the prison and the street bear a name with the noun *la santé*, meaning "health."

2. *Les porteurs de valises* ("the suitcase couriers"): The name given to the French living in France who supported militant Algerians in their struggle for Algerian independence. They often belonged to the clandestine network of Francis Jeanson, the founder of this support movement.

3. By moving from the singular pronoun *tu* to the plural *vous*, Omer angers Louis who feels that he is being placed in a category, with "all the French," a stereotype he refuses.

4. *Harki*s: Algerian auxiliary troops of the French army. The units

began as civilian self-defense groups. There was one unit per military sector in Algeria: Kabylia, the Aures, the Ouarsenis (58,000 *harki*s out of 263,000 auxiliary troops). Metropolitan French *harki*s: An auxiliary police force created by a statute of November 25, 1959 that was directed by Maurice Papon, head of the Paris police at that time. Recruited directly from Algeria, the corps of Algerian auxiliary troupes wore the blue uniforms of the Paris police and blue army caps.

5. FLN (National Liberation Front): The political organization that appeared on November 1, 1954, in Algeria. It carried out a series of attacks across the country specifically targeting the military and the police. Civilians were killed in the course of these attacks.

6. MNA (Algerian National Movement): Political organization founded by the Algerian nationalist, Messali Hadj, in December 1954. From 1955 to 1962, the FLN and the MNA fought one another to represent the Algerian people in Algeria as well as in France, among the immigrant population. Thousands died in the two countries.

7. The SAS (Special Administrative Sections): created by the municipal reform of 1956; they represented civil authority for 1,494 communities in Algeria and included approximately 1,200 officers.

8. *Hittistes:* A word derived from the Arabic word *hit* which means wall.

9. The GIA (Armed Islamic Groups): Defectors from the FIS, the Islamic Salvation Front, legalized by the Algerian government in September 1989. The GIA took responsibility for a certain number of assassinations of journalists, writers, and teachers.

10. *L'Aïd: L'Aïd al-Adha,* the feast of sacrifice, which in French is called "the feast of the sheep" and *Aïd al-Kabir,* the big feast: celebrated the tenth day of the twelfth month of the Muslim lunar calendar. Every Muslim family sacrifices a sheep that day to commemorate Abraham's sacrifice. The Muslim tradition considers Ismaël to be Abraham's oldest son and the first son to be circumcised.

11. Sebbar uses the phrase, "*C'est pacifique,*" which creates the play on words: *pacifique,* peaceful, and *Pacifique,* Pacific Ocean.

12. The French Federation of the FLN was an underground organization of Algerians living in France.

13. *Hallal:* What is permissible for a Muslim, specifically the meat of animals killed according to the Muslim ritual, by a Muslim. There are many *hallal* butcher shops in Paris and in several large French cities.

14. *Hijra:* The prophet Mohammed's exile from Mecca to Medina with a group of his faithful followers in 622. Threatened with death because of his preaching, the Prophet took refuge in Medina where he became the spiritual, political and military leader of Islam. The year 622

marks the beginning of the Muslim era and the Muslim calendar (1421 in the year 2000).

15. *Mujahidin:* Algerian rebels who fought against the French army for Algerian independence (1954–1962).

16. *Chechia:* red felt cap worn by men in North Africa.

17. *Houris:* Young virgins promised to good Muslims in paradise.

18. *Ninjas:* name given to Algerians in combat squads who wear black masks and black combat suits.

19. FFS: Socialist Forces Front. Political party founded in opposition to the FLN in 1963 by Hocine Aït Ahmed, one of the "historic leaders" of the Algerian war.

20. RCD (Rally for Culture and Democracy): The Algerian party opposing the FLN led by Saïd Saadi.

21. *Pieds noirs,* meaning "black" or "dark feet" is a term that refers to French citizens born in Algeria during the colonial period.

22. The CRS refers to the French security forces; the SS to the Nazi police.

23. Khaled is an Algerian singer popular in France as well as Algeria. He has been called the "King of Raï," a form of Algerian folk music. In this passage, music is audible from the nearby shops.

24. Johnny Halliday, the French rock and roll icon who became famous in the 1960s and is still performing today.

25. Slogan of the Banania brand of chocolate-based drinks and breakfast cereals. The logo used by this brand, featuring a smiling Senegalese infantry man, has been criticized by some in France and elsewhere as demeaning and a reflection of racist and colonialist attitudes in France.

26. *Fellouzes:* Pejorative term that refers to Algerian rebels. Derived from *fellaghas,* "peasants."

Works Cited

Brooks, Philip and Alam Hayling. 2001. *Une journée portée disparue. 17 octobre 1961* (film). France: Antenne 2. Originally presented as *Drowning by bullets*, UK: Channel 4, 1992.

Daenincx, Didier. 1984. *Meurtres pour mémoire.* Paris: Gallimard.

Djebar, Assia. 1985. *Fantasia, An Algerian Cavalcade.* Translated by Dorothy S. Blair. London and New York: Quartet Books. First published as *L'amour, la fantasia* (Paris: Jean Lattès, 1985; republished by Albin Michel, 1995).

Donadey, Anne. 1996. "'Une certaine idée de la France': the Algeria Syndrome and Struggles of 'French Identity,'" in *Identity Papers: Contested Nationhood in Twentieth Century France*, Steven Ungar and Tom Conley, eds., 215–232. Minneapolis: University of Minnesota Press.

———. 1999. "Between Amnesia and Anamnesis: Remembering the Fractures of Colonial History." *Studies in Twentieth Century Literature* 23/1: 111–116.

———. 2003. "Retour sur mémoire: La Seine était rouge de Leïla Sebbar," in *Leïla Sebbar*, Michel Laronde, ed., 187–198. Paris: L'Harmattan.

Einaudi, Jean-Luc. 1991. *La Bataille de Paris 17 octobre 1961.* Paris: Seuil.

Kettane, Nacer. 1985. *Le sourire de Brahim.* Paris: Denoël.

Lallaoui, Mehdi. 1986. *Les beurs de Seine.* Paris: L'Arcantère.

Laronde, Michel. 2007. "'Effets d'Histoire': Représenter l'Histoire coloniale forclose." *International Journal of Francophone Studies*, 10/1+2: 139–155.

Mattei, Georges M. 1982. *La guerre des gusses.* Paris: Balland.

Nora, Pierre. 1992. *Les lieux de mémoire.* Paris: Gallimard.

Rousso, Henry. 1987. *Le syndrome de Vichy (1944–198 . . .).* Paris: Seuil.

Sebbar, Leïla. 1990. "La Seine était rouge," in *Actualité de l'émigration hebdo*, 207: 14–16. Reprinted in *Le Maghreb Littéraire*, II:3 (1998): 95–98.

———. 1999. *La Seine était rouge*. Paris: Thierry Magnier.

———. 2003. *Je ne parle pas la langue de mon père*. Paris: Julliard.

———. 2004. *Mes Algéries en France*. Paris: Bleu autour.

———, and Nancy Huston. 1986. *Lettres parisiennes*. Paris: Bernard Barrault.

Stora, Benjamin. 2003. "La guerre d'Algérie dans les mémoires françaises: Violence d'une mémoire de revanche." Configurations of Memory in Postcolonial Narratives, *L'Esprit Créateur*, XVIII: 7–31.

Wiesel, Elie. 1989. *Silences et mémoire d'homme*. Paris: Seuil.

LEÏLA SEBBAR is one of the French-speaking world's most important writers. She was born in Algeria and lives in France. Her novels include *Je ne parle pas la langue de mon père; Marguerite; J.H. cherche âme-sœur;* and *Shérazade. The Seine Was Red* rewrites events that took place in Paris on October 17, 1961, when a peaceful protest organized by the Algerian Front de Libération Nationale was brutally suppressed by the police.

MILDRED MORTIMER is Professor of French at the University of Colorado in Boulder. She has translated Leïla Sebbar's *Le Silence des Rives/Silence on the Shores* and written several works on Francophone African literature, including *Journeys through the French African Novel; Writing from the Hearth: Public, Domestic, and Imaginative Space in Francophone Women's Fiction of Africa and the Caribbean;* and an edited work, *Maghrebian Mosaic: A Literature in Transition.*

CPSIA information can be obtained
at www.ICGtesting.com
Printed in the USA
JSHW051735070122
21842JS00001B/57

9 780253 220